The armored man looked very young, perhaps twenty-five—and Oriental, a remarkably rare pure genotype. The armor was dented, as if it had seen battle.

"How long have you been here?" Anna Nestor said. "You're no native. When did they capture you? Say something to us."

"My name is Kawashita Yoshio," he said. Nestor's translator analyzed his voice for planet and time period identification.

"He's Japanese," she read. "Twentieth century Earth."

"Earth." The full implication hit Elvox at once. "If you're right, he's the oldest living human—over 400 years. When were you born?"

"Christian year 1918," the man said.

"When were you captured?" Anna repeated.

"1942. Forgive me, but I also have many things to ask."

"Fair enough," Anna said. "You're very important now. You own this planet."

"Cannot own all this," Yoshio said. "*They* own it."

"*They're* gone. They took everything but you and your habitat."

"I am desolate," Yoshio said, hanging his head.

BEYOND HEAVEN'S RIVER

BEYOND HEAVEN'S RIVER

GREG BEAR

TOR

A TOM DOHERTY ASSOCIATES BOOK

BEYOND HEAVEN'S RIVER

Copyright © 1980 by Greg Bear

First Tor printing: January 1987

A TOR Book

Published by Tom Doherty Associates, Inc.
49 West 24 Street
New York, N.Y. 10010

Cover art by Ron Walotsky

ISBN: 0-812-53172-8
CAN. ED.: 0-812-53173-6

Printed in the United States of America

0 9 8 7 6 5 4 3 2 1

To my mother and father,
Dale and Wilma Bear

On the literary side,
this book is for Joseph
Conrad and Lafcadio Hearn.

ONE

Out of the parsec abyss came little more than the twenty-one centimeter whisper of hydrogen, God's favorite element. To the listeners, mechanical and human, it amounted to dead silence.

Alae Waunter entered the translucent blister of the Ear, rubbing sleep from her eyes. She put the equipment through several reference tests. Everything checked out. She frowned and replaced a short strand of reddish-brown hair.

A parsec away and over three years ago, the noise of an entire civilization had stopped. She tuned the Ear up and down the spectrum, passing the harsh whikker of the star, the cold murmurs of the outer gas giants in the solar system, the song of radiation trapped in ballooning magnetic fields. Then she focused, limiting her reception to the tiny point of the Perfidisian planet. There was nothing but cosmic background. They had been on station, listening through the Ear, for twenty-six years and nothing like this had ever happened before.

She flipped the switch which cut the Ear out of the circuits and altered reception to non-radiative communications. From the murmur of spaces below the Planck-Wheeler length came an even more profound silence.

Somehow, the Perfidisians had managed to blanket the most subtle signs of their presence. Or . . .

She froze. If something drastic had happened, they could be out of a contract, out of the work they had pursued for more than a quarter of a century.

Oomalo Waunter walked into the Ear naked, drying himself with a towel after a swim in the seatanks. He was the same height as his wife, with thin brown hair and pale skin. Despite his constant exercising, his body was smooth and faintly chubby. "What's up?" he asked.

Alae didn't answer. She took out special attachments and plugged them in one by one. The Ear expanded to thirty thousand times its usual size. The station's power sources whined faintly.

"I don't hear anything," she said.

"Let me give it a try." He repeated the tests she had made, then tried a few more. He checked the strain on their power sources and pulled the Ear in several thousand kilometers. "Sounds like an empty hunk of rock," he said. For all the time they had been on line, the Perfidisian planet—otherwise known only by a long serial number—had presented an image of heavy overbuilding, industry, mining, a general air of frantic if mysterious busyness.

The Perfidisians were unpredictable, prone to erratic migrations which no one had yet made any sense out of. Though the distant world had been their base of operations for over five thousand years, it wasn't inconceivable that they could have packed up and stolen away, even in so short a time as a day. Very little was known about them; the Waunters had never found out anything significant, nor, so far as they knew, had any of the other listeners spaced at even greater distances.

Alae moistened her lips and looked through the Ear's misty walls at the fog of stars. "If they're gone—" she began, her voice trembling.

"Shh. No." Oomalo put his hand on her shoulder. For weeks at a time they didn't touch each other, or see each other. The station was huge and they had worked out a routine over the years, leaving each other alone much of the time. But they had not grown apart. Oomalo sensed her distress and it made his stomach twist. "There may be more here," he continued. "I mean, it may be an opportunity."

They had relayed all they had heard for twenty-six years, so that their employers could feel that the puzzle of the Perfidisians was being solved, no matter how slowly. They had never known precisely who their employers were—the contract had been confirmed only on their end, with assurance in the form of credits formally registered and accepted by proxy twice yearly on Myriadne, Tau Ceti II.

"What kind of an opportunity?" she asked.

"Maybe they've left . . . that's possible. But if so, we're the first to know about it. There could be an entire planet down there, waiting for us, complete with artifacts."

Alae nodded. "I see that. What if they haven't left?"

"We take a risk."

Perfidisians had been known to go to great lengths to maintain their privacy. They were notorious for ruses, double blinds, and subtle violence—the kind of mishaps which couldn't be blamed on any particular party.

Alae didn't regret the decades spent on line. She felt no resentment—there had been no hardships. The work, in fact, had been ideally suited for them, bringing the peace they had never had working on other jobs. Before they had bought into the station—an old, reconditioned Aighor starship—they had spent the first five years of their marriage in miserable uncertainty, going after opportunities which had collapsed under them, twice declaring bankruptcy, with their equipment seized . . . All because they had taken chances, faced risks, and not been very lucky or smart. On line, whatever weaknesses had brought them to ruin so often were not in evidence. They had done their work well.

But still, hidden away was a yearning she would never rid herself of—thoughts of all the things they could have done, could have been.

It would be days before the next line of listeners noticed the change.

Opportunity.

Alae slapped a test module on the panel and pushed her way past Oomalo, walking down the oval corridor to the ship's old Aighor command center. Her footfalls were the only noise. She wanted to put her hands over her ears to hide from the silence. A quarter century of routine had made decisions agonizingly difficult. Oomalo followed. They sat in the twilight of the half-awake control consoles, smelling the dust and the cool electronic odors. Human-form chairs had been welded to the floor plates when the station had been re-outfitted, thirty years ago.

Most of the pathways and living quarters had been tailored for human occupation, but the command center was much as it had been for the past ten thousand years. The light on its consoles glowed with the same spectrum chosen by the last Aighors to crew the ship. Alien displays indicated that the dormant engines were still in working order.

They could be brought to life by touching three spots on a metal panel. The station could revert to a functioning starship in less than a minute. They could be in the Perfidisian system within a day. Within a day they could be dead, or they could count themselves among the wealthiest and most influential humans in the galaxy.

Alae glanced at her husband. "None of our risks were like this," she said. "Stakes were never so high."

He turned to the ancient position charts around the perimeter of the direct-view dome. "We've been here a long time," he said. "Perhaps long enough. If you think it's worth the risk."

Alae looked at the alien consoles with silver-flecked gray eyes, lips tight, one fist gripping and ungripping the fabric of her pants. "Let's start before the others learn."

Oomalo leaned forward and pulled a plastic cloth away from the console. An amber metal plate with sixty symbols glinted in the red light of the slumbering monitors. He touched two of the symbols. The console brightened. A human computer had been interfaced with the old Aighor machine. "We're going to enter the Perfidisian system," Oomalo told the computer. He consulted more up-to-date charts on his tapas, a small personal computer, then gave the tag-numbers and geodesics to follow. The computer translated. The old ship made hollow, resentful noises, but it complied. Their view of the stars in the direct-view dome was cut off.

Before pressing the third symbol, Oomalo broadcast a formal message to their employers, severing the listening contract.

There was an old, established law. The first beings to set foot on a world not inhabited (or likely to be inhabited) by other intelligent beings could claim the world for themselves, or for the interests they represented. Nothing in their contract held them to *represent* their employers.

The Perfidisians were among the most powerful, and certainly the most mysterious, species in the Galaxy. Information about them would command enormous prices. And the Waunters would command the information.

The old ship went above space-time as smoothly as a

leviathan through arctic seas. For three hours there was nothing around them; the ship was their universe. It was at least ten thousand years old, from the third-stage Aighor civilization, and a sizable three kilometers from bow to stern. They had purchased it at auction from Crocerian free merchants. Oomalo sat in the human-form chair, watching the dreams higher spaces always coaxed from his mind. Matter behaved with subtle differences when removed from the reassurance of its natural realm. In grossly tuned bodies like a ship's hull, the effect was minimal, but computers had to be adjusted to override dangerous errors and misconceptions. The human brain and the nerves of the body were self-adjusting over periods of several minutes, but vague distortions and fancies washed over a person and made concentration difficult. Some experienced ecstasies, others nightmares.

Alae Waunter gripped her chair arms tightly, face rigid, eyes pressed shut. Her pupils twitched behind closed lids. She was lost in a quandary of choices. After so many years, she could hardly imagine having power over other people, having *influence*. Perhaps it would be the same as never being ignored, never being bothered for petty reasons, never disdained. When she spoke, others would listen. She had never been influential before coming on line. She had never had much of anything before the partnership and marriage, before the ship. Together they had earned a good living, but there was something more . . .

Blue skies. Beautiful places to live, human places. Spacious houses without ship noises. Sometimes she felt she was becoming an Aighor, surrounded by so much that was non-human. But making choices had always bothered her. So much to lose. So often, they had lost. For a time she had believed something powerful and invisible had been appointed to punish them, discourage them, because they had not been daring enough. Now they were daring. Now they would fly right into the realm of the Perfidisians, and they would possibly die—or worse—would discover that the Perfidisians, or some power like them, had been the appointed discouragers all along. She tensed. A small back portion of her mind pursued the idea, flinging out vision after vision of a Perfidisian hell, cages with sticks being poked incessantly, escape opportunities turning into more chances for failure, orchestrated failure and disappointment. Her arm muscles knotted. Until now, at least they had had peace. How foolish to risk peace for the chance of cages and sticks, mud on their faces as they crawled away and were captured. How foolish even in the face of influence, beating the odds, blue skies and fine places to live. She should have thought it out more carefully, but it was too late now. The decision had been made.

Oomalo unstrapped himself and made his way carefully to relief facilities. There he defecated, washed, and ordered a meal. He didn't bother to ask if Alae needed anything. Warping was a brief visit to her own private hell, and it was impolite to disturb someone so involved.

He felt mildly drunk. He leaned against the wall outside the relief center and ate a piece of bread, eyes almost closed. He wondered what it would be like to have trillions of words of desired information to sell. But his fancies were vaguely boring. He had never disliked life aboard the station. It was comfortable, secure, and interesting. He could spend many more decades exploring the old ship, adding to his picture of the civilization that had built it. Being rich probably wouldn't give him problems any more interesting than the ones he already had.

But he respected Alae's decisions. She had decided to contract-purchase the old ship and offer it as a listening station so close to the Perfidisian system. Her offer had been snatched up quickly by their employers, and the ship had been paid off and signed over to the Waunters for a thirty-year contract, with reversion after twenty-five years. The ship was technically theirs now. And it was due to her that his life was as interesting as it was. He knew exactly what he offered her in return: a means to give her plans solidity.

The period ended none too soon for Alae. The ship fell from strangeness, and the direct-view bubble cleared. Stars and clouds of stars, perspectives almost unchanged, waited as always. She pressed her temples and nodded as if to sort her tumbling memories back into place. Then the hell passed and she stood to go with Oomalo to the Ear.

Silence still. They put the ship into a long, cautious orbit, down to the tiny pinprick that was the Perfidisian planet.

From a thousand kilometers the surface was gray and

blue, splotched with rust-red and bands of ochre. It was covered with a cross-thatch of what may have been roads at one time. No natural landscape remained, and no prominent artificial structures. Everything had been scoured away, leaving the surface reasonably smooth, with no irregularities greater than four to five meters. Alae shot the sunlit crescent during one orbit, and swept microwave and other sensors from pole to pole. There was mild weather but no oceans; updrafts but no mountains; oxygen but no plant life. No life at all.

"They made sure we wouldn't find anything obvious," Oomalo said.

Alae cleared her throat and put the instruments on deep-crust scan. "Either that, or they're masking it," she said. "It's hard to believe they'd take the time to wipe a world clean."

"Hard to believe they'd run away from a world in the first place," Oomalo said. "But they have."

The horizon scanner chirruped, and Alae aimed the display projector at her retina. "There's one thing left," she said. "A dome structure, about as large as our ship."

"That's it?"

"Standing alone on a smooth plain."

"That's where we land," Oomalo said. Alae agreed with a nod, and they prepared a tiny probe for the first surface venture. While Alae fueled the device, Oomalo went to get the lander ready. They dropped the ship into a tighter orbit and released the probe into the atmosphere. The probe's cameras recorded the area around the dome during its descent. The pictures were monotone and conveyed little more information than was obtained in scans from high orbit. The dome was featureless, three thousand five hundred and sixty-one meters in diameter, surrounded by a plain of concretelike material.

Alae took a deep breath to subdue her spookiness. Everything was going too smoothly. She wasn't apprehensive about being trapped—they'd already come too close to worry about that. But a third alternative was becoming depressingly clear.

There might not be anything left to bother with.

The probe set down without incident. It scanned the featureless hemisphere in three sweeps, two vertical and one horizontal. The dome's perfect outline was distorted slightly by internal supports—a deviation of one or two centimeters where they touched the interior.

"Structure is sound," the computer announced. "It isn't designed with much flair or efficiency."

"What's it made of?" Alae asked.

The probe shot a tiny charge of superheated gas into the dome and analyzed the spectrum from the resulting flash of light. "Structure is largely glass, with filaments of boron laced through it. There are traces of lead and molybdenum."

The probe's signal faded as they slipped into the planet's shadow. There were no belts of trapped particles, no way to analyze the atmospheric effluent of the vanished Perfidisians. The air was very weak but pure. The planet was cold and asleep. There were only slight gravitational anomalies associated with plate tectonics and the building of mountain chains—but there were no mountains. Alae guessed they had been condensed, not scraped or blown away but simply pressed into conformity with a desired reference level.

The swaths of red and ochre were due to impurities of iron and copper in the artificial surface, probably caused by percolation of groundwater through the porous material.

Monotonous. Empty. Alae's face was tight, and she pressed her teeth together grimly. It might be their world now, but it was no treasure trove. She released some tension in a ragged sigh. Her neck muscles were tightening. She abhorred the idea of letting the medical units calm her down, but if she got any more wound up she'd have to. She almost wished everything were back to normal. Wanting something so badly and not being sure it even existed was more distressing than anything she'd felt for decades. The routine of the station had seeped into her body and thoughts, and she had no defenses against overreacting.

"Med unit," she said softly.

"This device will summon," the computer replied. The smooth jade-green ceiling had been equipped with tracks. Two medical units, cubes hanging from slender chrome poles, beeped behind her.

"Bring me down to relaxed and alert," she said. "No impairment of CNS." She stood and held an arm out to the nearest cube. The second cube advanced and flashed lights in her eyes. She felt a prick in the skin above her bicep. Her neck muscles loosened, and she was calm.

"Med unit suggests a brief training regimen to establish complete CNS control of emotional responses," the computer said.

"Noted. How's he doing with the lander?"

"It's ready," Oomalo said behind her.

"Then let's go down."

From outside, a view they hadn't seen since being positioned for listening, the old Aighor ship looked like an asteroid carved from malachite. It was flattened, twice as long as it was wide, and featureless except for the bumps and gouges covering its surface. It had been through at least a dozen major battles in its prime, with countless wounds inflicted by unknown weapons, some large enough to have required rebuilding the ship in deep space. The repaired sections were detectable only where they obviously deviated from the original design of the ship.

The lander turned its thrust nodes against the orbital path and let loose a steady wash of rainbow light. The vessel shuddered and G-forces increased. They began to spiral in.

Pearls and dust, everything leeched of color. Ice-crystal clouds formed a thin haze at thirty kilometers. The lander punched through them and thrust again. It touched down half a kilometer from the dome. The surface under its engines cooled immediately. A quarter kilometer away, a few patches of snow liquefied, then turned to glassy ice.

They put on full suits before opening the hatch. A ramp flowed from the outer wall, and they walked down to the plain. Their radios whistled, and the voice of the station computer announced that two other ships had entered orbits around the planet.

"Nothing we can do about it now," Oomalo said. "Send a record of our prior landing to Centrum Archive. To our employers send a note that we are accepting bids for data mining on this world. We are sole owners."

They approached the dome. From this side there was no visible entrance. They marched around it. Oomalo kept his suit recorders on throughout the walk. On the dome's north side they came across a door. It was round and three meters high. A black spiral in the middle wound to a red depression that was obviously meant to be touched. Oomalo pushed it with a gloved hand. The door vanished.

"It's fast," Alae said. "I barely saw it flash aside." They entered. It was warmer inside, and the air was thicker, richer in oxygen and nitrogen. The door was closed behind them when they turned to look.

They were in a peristyle. Five meters above them a roof jutted from the inside of the dome. To either side it extended around the curve, making a circuit. They stepped from the roof's shadow and stood under the nighttime sky, with stars and the outlines of clouds. Directly before them was a grassy hill dotted with broad, dark trees. Beyond the hill was a tower, multistoried and ornate, like several houses stacked atop each other. Climbing the hill, they came to a path, beside which stood a stone lantern with a cap which resembled the roof of the tower. A body lay on the path, pushed against the base of the lantern.

"It looks human," Oomalo said, turning it faceup with the toe of his boot. A few seconds after he touched it, it crumbled into white powder. Only its clothing and armor remained. The armor was made of shiny black metal and beautifully decorated, like the carapace of an insect.

Alae bent to pick up a sword she'd stepped on. She held it out for Oomalo to examine. "These are human artifacts," she said. She shined her suit lamp into the dark at the top of the hill. Something moved. "They're not all dead," she said. Oomalo nodded behind his faceplate, and they walked to the top.

From that vantage they could see that the dome was a terrarium, designed to mimic a terrestrial landscape. On the other side of the hill was a village, with buildings made of wood and a thin, translucent material, illuminated by spots of straw-colored light. Everything was silent and still.

Alae had never been to Earth, but she'd experienced enough tapes to know it like a native. "It's summer here," she said.

"Dead summer," Oomalo added, coming across another body. He didn't touch this one but bent over and shined his suit lamp into the face. "These were never alive. They must have been simulacra." The hair had been pulled back on the scalp to form a short topknot. The clothing was voluminous and comfortable-looking. The eyes were closed and the face was peacefully composed, but the back of the head had already begun to powder from the body's weight.

They walked around a stone wall until they came to a gate, which stood open. They entered the compound and approached the tower. A square doorway beckoned at the base of the imposing wooden structure. Oomalo stepped up to look inside.

A shadow jumped into the doorway with sword raised. Oomalo held up his arm and stepped back. They stood two paces apart. The figure wore a fierce metal mask. Oomalo stepped back again, and it advanced aggressively.

"Dare ni aitai n desu ka?" it said.

"What?" Alae asked.

"Dare?"

Oomalo held out one hand and reached up to draw aside his face plate. "We're like you," he said. He heard the voice of the station computer in Alae's helmet, and hints of her whispered reply. Then she slid aside her own faceplate and held her hands out, palms up.

"Nippongo wa yoku dekimasen," she said. "We don't speak Japanese."

The figure sagged and lowered its sword. In a flash it sheathed the blade, opened its helmet from the front, and removed it. "Forgive me," the man said, bowing quickly. "I have been here a long time. Forgive me very much."

TWO

Alae put the portable environment pack on the ground beside the armored man and looked up at the descending point of light. Oomalo joined them, and the dome hatch shut swiftly behind. "Take him to our ship?" Alae asked.

"Let the others take care of him," he said. "We have to establish our claim now."

The armored man stared steadily at the ground and took a deep breath.

"You mean he has a claim?"

"That's what it amounts to. He was here before us."

"That's insane."

"This is going to be contested by everyone who sets foot here. We just keep silent and maybe things will work out for us. But we don't dare touch him or we'll be accused of—"

Even through the bubble of air around them, the sound of the landing craft drowned out his voice. Alae's gray eyes looked over the armored man coldly.

"Let's go, then," she said. They resealed their suits and slipped out of the bubble.

The second shuttle's engines had stopped. There was a mark on its side Oomalo didn't recognize, though it bore a resemblance to the family crest of a man he had once free-lanced for—Traicom Nestor. Alae boarded their lander ahead of him. The ramp swung inboard just as another piercing whine cut through the thin atmosphere.

"What's her registry?" Oomalo asked, going to the shuttle's computers and calling up lists of symbols. Alae watched over his shoulder. "Anna Sigrid Nestor," he said finally. "United Stars won't be far behind. Finalists into the stretch."

The second shuttle's outer shields flickered off, and a ramp swung out from the base. Immediately a bubble of air poked down and nestled around the landing vanes. A crowd of humans in colorful costumes exited from the cargo lock. For a moment it looked like a circus had come to the Perfidisian planet. The passengers milled in the environment bubble, blinking in the washed-out light, adjusting their elegant capes and swirling ropes. The austere black and gray suits of three androgynes stood out, along with the russet fur of several tecto alters. One last figure, a woman in an orange and red gown, watched from the top of the ramp, carrying her own environment pack.

The third ship landed in a copper halo of light.

The woman in orange and red nodded to someone behind her and stepped down into the crowd of twenty passengers. She left the bubble and began walking over the featureless pavement to the dome, skirting the Waunters' lander.

The third ship dropped a ramp, and immediately a tall, well-muscled man with bright red hair ran out of lock. He was wearing the uniform of a United Stars loytnant. His environment trailed after him with some difficulty as he ran to catch up with the woman. Breathless, he merged his bubble with hers, and they walked on together.

She paid him no attention. "Heiress, have you riddled what I've riddled?" he asked nervously.

"No riddles," she replied. "Plain as sky. I'm going to talk to the owner of this planet." She was well formed but not exceptionally beautiful, not to his eyes at that moment, with a hard-edged, masculine face, large eyes, arched brows indicating amusement, narrow jaw, and a sensuous mouth.

"I'm Elvox," the man said. "Julio Elvox, senior officer in charge of this landing."

"Good for you," the woman said.

"And I recognize you—you're Anna Nestor."

She nodded and arched one brow further, but still didn't look at him. They were approaching the dome.

"We don't know who he is," Elvox said, indicating the man, "or where he came from."

"Nor I. Shall we be careful and courteous?"

"What language does he speak?"

"I haven't any idea. I've got a translator tapas with me. I suppose you do, too. If he speaks any terrestrial language, we'll understand each other."

"You're sure he's human?" Elvox asked.

Anna Nestor gave him an amused, ironic smile, looking him over for the first time with a single up-and-down scan. She nodded to herself as if making a note. "You're only a loytnant," she said.

Elvox opened his mouth to reply but nothing came out.

The armored man watched without apparent interest as they approached him. "Careful," Elvox said. "He's wearing a sword and another knife." The armor was dented as if it had seen combat. The three environment bubbles merged, and Anna stopped a few paces in front of the man.

"Hello," she greeted him casually. He turned his forlorn face toward her and blinked, but said nothing. He looked very young, perhaps twenty-five—a few years younger than Nestor or Elvox. His skin was light brown and his eyes were black, with epicanthic folds, which marked him as a fairly pure Oriental. Racial purity wasn't unheard of on human worlds, but it was rare enough for remark. "How long have you been here?" He didn't answer. He seemed lost in some inner tragedy.

Anna looked his costume over.

"If that's an example of Perfidisian daily wear—assuming he's been held prisoner or under study—they must be pretty limited in their technology," Elvox said.

"It's beautiful," Anna said. "He's no native."

"Then they captured him," Elvox said.

Nestor looked at the loytnant as if he wasn't entirely useless. "When?"

"A long time ago. Perhaps a thousand years."

"Where did they catch him?"

"Earth." The full implications hit them both at once.

"If you're right, he's the oldest living human," Anna said. "He's valuable regardless of this planet. Say something to us," she addressed the armored man, pretending to drag words from her mouth with a hand.

"My name is Kawashita Yoshio," he said. His English was doubly accented, by time and by the fact that it wasn't his native tongue, which made him hard to understand. Nestor's translator tapas went to work and described his nationality and time period.

"He's Japanese," she read from the display. "Twentieth century."

"His clothes put me off five hundred years," Elvox said.

"Yes, Japanese," the man affirmed. "For you, my first name is Yoshio, my family name Kawashita."

"When were you born?" Elvox asked.

"Christian year one thousand nine hundred and eighteen."

"When were you captured?" Nestor asked.

"Christian year one thousand nine hundred and forty-two."

"Where?"

He shook his head and glanced between them, then looked down at his feet. "Forgive me, do not wish to offend, but I have many things of asking, perhaps will trade, point for point, *neh*?"

"Fair enough," Nestor said. "You'll have to understand the situation clearly before you make any commitments." She pressed her tapas and the device translated her speech into Japanese. "You're very important now. Many people will want to talk to you."

"Why?" he asked. "I have lost."

"By no means," Nestor said. "You're very lucky. You probably own this planet now."

"He may not know what that means," Elvox said.

"I am not ignorant," Yoshio said defensively. "I was let to read, many years."

"It means that for a time you were the only being on this world. That probably makes you the owner."

"Cannot own all this," Yoshio said. "They own it."

"They're gone." Nestor swept her arms around the empty prairies of concrete. "They took everything but you and your habitat."

"I am desolate," Yoshio said, hanging his head. "I have lost."

Nestor and Elvox looked at each other with obvious questions. The man was unable to fend for himself. Who would be his adviser and guardian?

"There's not much you can objectively do for Yoshio Kawashita," she said in a formal tone. "You represent a consolidation with concerns of its own."

"And you don't?" Elvox said, indignant.

"I didn't say that. I'm just excusing myself if I look after his interests before you do." She extended her bubble to encompass Yoshio's, picked up the portable environment pack the Waunters had left near him, and grasped his arm gently. "Come with me." He did as he was told. Their environments broke away from Elvox's with an audible pop. Elvox frowned, seeing his promotion march away after them.

THREE

Kawashita looked over the lander's interior without much surprise. It was more precisely fashioned, with fewer jutting pipes and beams, but essentially it was little different from the inner spaces of the *Hiryu*. He wasn't very clear on what the ship did, but it was obviously a ship.

As for the woman who escorted him, she behaved like a man, and that in itself told him things were different here. The varieties of people in the entourage, now waiting in the ship's small cargo area, meant little to him, so he ignored them—all except one who was covered with fur. He felt a tingle go up his back as if he'd seen a demon.

"My name is Anna Sigrid Nestor," the woman told him. "You're in a landing vehicle which will take us up to a larger ship in a few days. If you don't want to be here, if you don't want to go with us, tell me now and we'll put you back on the field or in your dome."

Kawashita thought that over for a few seconds. "No," he said. "I've been there too long."

"I'll say," Nestor sighed. "Four hundred years."

"Many lifetimes. I was many things there, learned many things."

'We'll also need your permission to record everything we do with you. We don't want to be accused of kidnapping or anything illegal."

"How . . . record?"

She held up the tapas pad. "Everything we do and say is kept in the pad's memory, and temporarily in the lander's computer, too. I imagine all this is unfamiliar to you."

"I was let to read," Kawashita said.

"Do we have your permission?"

"To record, yes," he said.

"Would you like to rest, change clothes?"

He held up his arms and let them drop. Metal and heavy cloth shuffled together. "Show me clothes."

She motioned for the entourage to stay back and took him to a private cabin. "You can take your pick of any of these outfits. Some are designed to snug-fit once they're worn, but they aren't the best-looking in the lot." He looked through the small closet and felt for supports above the clothing. They were floating free. He didn't remark on it. Instead, he sadly and deliberately picked out a gray and green robe with baggy pants and a belt. It was something he could get used to. Many of the others were rather disturbing.

"Well." Nestor sighed again. "Congratulations. You've picked one that'll snug fit. I imagine you're modest, so you can dress in here"—she pointed to a separate bathroom— "while I wait outside."

"I'm not so modest," Kawashita said. "But wait outside anyway."

"Of course. Where did you learn English?"

"I was let to read."

"Of course." She smiled and backed out, the door sliding shut behind her.

It was pleasant to be alone, even in a strange place. He'd almost become used to living alone—except for Ko, of course. He put the costume down on a bunk and looked at the cabin and the bathroom. He could learn much from simple fixtures, if he only knew how to interpret them. Some might be dangerous. Some might look innocuous but be very important. While he removed his armor and clothing, he whistled tunelessly. He put his bearskin shoes together next to the bunk, then removed the gauntlets from his arms. The lacquered plates rattled against each other as he arranged them on a chair. With some difficulty he reached behind himself to undo the cords and remove his breastplate. He slipped off his *hitatare*, which in the rush to get suited he had stolen from the body of a low-ranking samurai. Some white powder filtered from the shoulders.

It would take some time for his hair to grow out, he decided as he looked at the bathroom mirror. He rubbed his scalp, and the mirror flashed a question mark in one corner. He ignored it. While he figured out how to use the urinal, a voice asked what he wanted. He looked at the walls but said nothing as he used the facilities. They were relatively easy to understand. One of the fixtures looked obscene—an obvious phallus and less obvious but identifiable female genitalia formed in plastic and mounted on a smooth black cylinder next to the washbasin. Above the basin, next to the mirror, was a black cube with many little doors outlined on its surfaces. He looked at himself in the mirror, and again it flashed a question mark.

"Do you desire scalp massage?" the voice asked.

"No," he said.

"Does your hair need treatment?"

He shook his head. "Needs to grow."

"This machine will adjust style by request." The black cube turned red, then went back to black. He wasn't ready to take that kind of risk. He refused as politely as he could—there might, after all, be an actual human somewhere behind the walls—and put on the pants and robe. The pants shrunk appreciably until they weren't baggy, just comfortably loose. The robe adjusted in a similar fashion. Looking in the mirror, bare chest peeking out between the lapels of the robe, he thought he had made a good compromise.

If this was his cabin, he was much better off than he'd been in the bunkroom aboard the *Hiryu*. He frowned and picked up his armor, adjusting it and sticking it into the closet, where something invisible held it in place. His clothing was ragged, so he left it out to be mended or thrown way.

"Ko," he said, looking around the cabin. "Where are you?" He smiled and nodded at the opposite wall. "It is good of you to come with me. In a while, we will talk. But now they wait." His face sagged into a frown. "So many years, and now there are others, real people. So strange. I think much has changed, and I may never know how much. What? Yes, nothing will be the same now. The *kami* have left in anger and shame, they will not return. We deserve our confusion. Now hide again. I will call the woman and go with her."

He went to the door and opened it. "I am ready," he said.

Anna looked over his clothing and nodded appreciatively. "Not bad." She stepped through the door and looked around the cabin. "Are you ready to meet someone who actually speaks Japanese? She doesn't even need a tapas. I'll introduce you."

"Is it common tongue?" he asked.

"No, not exactly."

"Then I speak English when possible."

"That'll disappoint our linguist. She knows forty old human languages, and she likes to practice. But you know best."

"I know Chinese, Tagalog, and some Malay," he said. "Are those common?"

"Chinese is spoken widely but probably not as you remember it. Better stick with English for the time being. Your accent isn't too thick to penetrate, and English hasn't changed much in grammar and syntax since it was standardized, about a century and a half after you—" She lifted her hand. "After whatever happened."

"I will tell," he said. "But first I need food, and a tour."

"By all means," she said. "If you'll be patient, we'll take you up to the big ship. With permission, of course."

"Up?" he asked. He pointed his finger meekly.

"To orbit. To a warper ship—a space vessel."

"Space," he repeated. "This is a ship for space?"

Nestor nodded. "We have a lot to explain, I can see that."

"This is not the Earth?" He had suspected as much, but now he wanted to be sure.

She shook her head gently. "Earth is very, very far away."

"Then I am glad," he said. "Have not lost as much as was thought."

"If you're ready, a few of my friends would like to meet you."

"Ones with fur and bright clothes?"

"No, not right now. You can meet them later if you want. I have a first officer who's very good at history. She tells me you were dressed as a samurai warrior, but that you're not from that time period. You've made us all very curious."

"Will speak for exchange," Kawashita said, his lips thinning with determination. "You will tell and let me read all I have to know about this." He gestured vaguely at the bulkheads.

"Of course. In a few days you'll get to talk to people

from the Centrum. They'll probably assign someone to look after your welfare. If you wish, you can leave with them. But for the moment you're welcome here."

"First, food."

"Come along." Nestor opened the door and he stepped cautiously into the corridor, which circled the periphery of the lander. She stood him on a black spot beneath a hole and told him to keep his arms down. They were lifted gently to the next level. Yoshio reflexively clutched at the passing walls, sucking in his breath through his teeth. Anna touched his shoulder. "Don't worry," she said.

They stepped out of the lift field. Walking away from the periphery—Yoshio tried to orient himself, and decided they were moving toward the center of the ship—they came to a small cabin with two round tables. Four pearl-like spheres, each about forty centimeters wide, hung without apparent support just beneath the ceiling. A bright, lively painting of a strange jungle covered one wall. At least, Yoshio mused, it wasn't a photograph—it was three-dimensional, very detailed, and seemed in constant motion.

"What would you like to eat?" Anna asked. She pointed to a square in the table nearest them. He sat down and looked into the square. Pictures of food flashed past, and hints of odor, as well as taste. He backed away, sucked in his breath—"Hht!"—then leaned forward more slowly. Some of the tastes were unfamiliar, even unpleasant.

"You can look at it again if you want, just ask for a re-run."

"Yes," Yoshio said. "Again, please." The menu passed again. He settled for what looked like a plate of fish and reasonably unaltered vegetables. He then chose a drink very close to beer, and ignored a list of supplementary nourishment. "What is the third list for?" he asked.

"Some of my crew have religious regimens which require special diets to be effective," she said. "Some are on selective starvation diets, others modified intoxicants, and that means they need periodic supplements to keep them healthy." She pointed to the tapas, which had been silent for the past few minutes, and asked if he needed translation any longer.

He shook his head. "I would rather hear people speak and understand. Explain odd words to me, or give me dictionary."

"Here." She handed over the tapas. He hefted the device and looked at its pale gray screen. It fit easily into the palm of his hand. "Simply punch these three buttons in sequence and speak an unfamiliar word into the face. The screen will give a written translation in Japanese."

While he tested the pad, his food drifted down from an opening in one of the spheres and his drink rose up from the table, glass and all. He tasted the beer and smiled slightly. "It is like San Miguel," he said. "Philippines beer."

"We try," Anna said. "If that means it's good."

"Yes," Yoshio said.

Anna leaned back in the chair as he ate. "Would you like to know what you're eating? Might be a good place to start asking questions."

Kawashita held a bite of food in mid-air and looked at it suspiciously. "This is not fish?" he asked.

"We don't kill animals for food anymore. It's generically known as synthecarn. It's artificial, but I doubt you can tell the difference. Some of us object to it because it looks like dead animal flesh, but that's a pretty fine distinction. The vegetables are cloned products grown in a few seconds in special containers. Most of what you're eating was a liquid nutrient solution a few minutes ago, and reclaimed waste products before that."

"The future is not appetizing," Kawashita said. But he took a bite of the fish and decided it was acceptable. "And the beer?"

"Artificial. I'm not sure how it's produced."

"Do people anywhere eat things as I once did?"

"Probably. There are quite a few colony worlds where people have chosen to go back to old ways—maybe five or six thousand. But most are more rational. This is much more efficient, and just as satisfactory to anyone but a zealot."

Kawashita took the pad and said, "Cloned." Writing appeared and continued for several minutes, moving at an easy pace across the tapas screen. "I will not need a library with this," he said.

"It is a library. Don't get too dependent on it, though. We have a clinical name for people who can't stay away from a tapas."

"Tapas," Kawashita said to himself. "In Sanskrit it means heat."

"We get it from a MitelAllemain root. MitelAllemain—"

"Middle German," Kawashita translated.

"Yes. It's a language used on colony worlds with mixes of French-, German-, and English-speaking peoples. There's another form called PlatAllemain, which has Spanish and Russian influences, and a third called Soyuvet, which is mostly Russian and a few other Slavic tongues. But they're not standard. Centrum English and Demotiki—that's mostly Greek, I think—are quite common. Most people are willing to speak English, unless you're in political situations where native tongues are important. You seem to be a natural—knowing Sanskrit, translating quasi-French and German."

"Many years of study when let alone, when let to read. I know only bits and fragments. You seem to have easy ways to learn languages, however. Could I be taught?" He was almost finished with his meal.

"I don't see why not. Would you like to meet the others now?"

"First, a tour," he said.

"Fine." She smiled broadly. "You're a hard bargainer."

FOUR

Elvox had requested historical records from the orbiting United Stars ship. Displaying them rapidly and running an automatic search, he found no listing for a terrestrial citizen named Yoshio Kawashita. But the records were incomplete before 1990. He shrugged and handed the display tapas to his second-in-command, a heavyset unterloytnant, Lawrence Tivvers. Tivvers replayed the search and agreed with the negative results.

"I don't think they'll coerce him," Elvox said. "We could prove illegal persuasion in any judgment dispute. But he's open game for any kind of persuasion. He's naive."

"All this is on the fringes of the law," Tivvers said, clearing the outside view ports to see the woman's shuttle and the dome. "But it's pretty clear, even so. He's inherited the planet."

"And we can't investigate a damned thing unless he gives us permission."

Tivvers punched up their work schedule and began to revise it. "I think we're going to have to freeze everything until the Centrum ship gets here." The Centrum oversaw the actions of mercantile consolidations like United Stars, and mediated when disputes arose. "USC won't like us taking chances with a punitive decision."

"Larry, I blew my chances for a promotion out there."

"How? By not taking him in? That may work against her."

"She's too smart to do anything that will work against her. But she's getting friendly with him, and we're out in the cold."

"Wait until the Centrum arrives. We'll get our orders from the CO next accession, ten minutes from now—patience!"

Elvox rubbed his face. "She stepped right in, no weaknesses, no doubts. She swept him away like a storm. I didn't have a chance to think."

Tivvers acknowledged a beep on the intercom.

"Sir, this is Ruysmal. We're ready to examine the dome."

"Hold off on that," Elvox said. "We're going to sit tight for a while." He slapped his palm on a panel and stood. "That's timid, isn't it? Would she be timid?"

Tivvers looked at him, a faint grin surfacing.

"She wouldn't be timid, would she?"

"Hell, no. She's Anna Nestor."

"She's no older than I am, no more experienced."

"No," Tivvers mused, "not in this sort of thing, maybe."

"You believe all those stories about her?"

Tivvers' grin was open now.

"She's something to go up against, you know that? If we sit tight, she's going to run circles around us."

"You're not thinking about taking chances, are you?"

"How did the CO get his command?"

Tivvers shook his head. "Julio, that was thirty years ago, things were different. The Centrum controls the show now. No consolidation dares go up against the Centrum—not when every other consolidation will jump all over its ass. This is a time of honor and decorum."

Elvox made a rude noise, then punched up the cargo lock. "Ruysmal, get your team out to the dome and go over it with every detector we have. Don't disturb anything, but find out everything you can." He squeezed past Tivvers and took the ladder to the next deck, his voice rising up the shaft. "She can't refuse to let me see him. They'll say she was holding him out of communication. She has to let me talk to him."

"Julio, before we do anything, let's at least see what the legal advisers have to say."

The sound of Elvox's steps on the ladder stopped. "Okay. But make it quick. I'm getting a pack ready."

FIVE

Elvox crossed the field, rehearsing what he would say and how he would behave. Anna Nestor was an imposing figure, but this was too important to allow himself to be cowed. As he neared her shuttle, Tivvers told him by radio that the legal advisers concurred.

"Good," he breathed. "Now I hope the CO goes along with me, too."

"He will, if you succeed," Tivvers said.

"Succeed at what? I'm not even sure what I'm after."

"Influence, sir. Make him think we're friendly, too. We can help."

"Clear enough." He closed the channel and opened another to talk with Nestor's shuttle. His environment merged with the bubble around the base of the lander.

"Can we help you?"

He looked up and saw a tecto alter standing in the cargo-lock hatch. Nestor seemed to have a fair number of alters in her entourage. Usually, alters chose to stay with their own kind—in societies of less than a thousand, since there were seldom more than that number of any particular type. Elvox didn't approve of adaptive breeding and tectonogenetics programs, personally, but USC did, and he was loyal to USC. "I'd like to speak to Anna Nestor."

"And you're"—the alter consulted a tapas—"Loytnant Elvox, correct?"

He nodded. The alter stepped back into the lock, leaving Elvox to rub his hands at the base of the ramp.

"Loytnant Elvox," Nestor's voice ran out from the outside speaker. "Come aboard, and be welcome."

"Thank you," he murmured.

The alter took him to the lander's bridge. Nestor and several others were giving Kawashita rudimentary instruction on the state of modern technology. He referred to a tapas frequently. Elvox made a mental note to subpoena that tapas in any legal dispute, to see if it was biased.

The Japanese seemed at ease. He was listening studiously to everything said, though he couldn't possibly understand a tenth of it, Elvox thought.

Anna took Elvox aside and welcomed him aboard the ship. "What can we do for you, Loytnant?"

"I'm here to speak with Kawashita, find out how he came to be here, offer him our congratulations . . ." He trailed off and smiled nervously. Kiril Kondrashef, Nestor's shuttle pilot, was explaining the craft's power system. Anna turned away to explain a detail more simply. She then turned back to Elvox and motioned him to take a seat.

"We're very interested in your welfare, Yoshio," Elvox said during a lull. "As . . . uh . . . Anna Nestor is. And we want you to understand how important your position is now." Nestor smiled enigmatically. Elvox suddenly felt like a clumsy child.

"I begin to see," Kawashita said. "Things are being explained well."

"I hope you see that there are a great many things that will be very difficult for you to understand . . . right away." He smiled ingratiatingly at Nestor, by way of experiment. Her smile shifted slightly and seemed to mirror his own. "Our technology is too complex for even a modern individual to absorb quickly. Some of the concepts will probably take years to sink in."

"Probably," Kawashita admitted. "I am not unfamiliar with some, however. Was talked about for a long time, this warper ability."

Elvox was taken aback. "In your time, they . . . uh . . . knew about higher and lower spaces, how to use them?"

Kawashita shook his head. "Not in my time. After. I was let to read."

Elvox itched to ask what he had been allowed to read, but a glance at Nestor told him the Japanese wasn't willing to divulge such things yet. She shook her head and pursed her lips.

"Yoshio is up on quite a few things we wouldn't expect him to be," she said. "He's learning very quickly."

The lander shuddered slightly, and a mournful hum vibrated through the bulkheads. The pilot cleared the direct-view plates. Dark thunderheads were piling up all around the dome and landing area. Elvox saw Ruysmal and Dean walking toward the dome, leaning into a stiff breeze.

"Looks like the Waunters are settling in for a blow," the pilot said.

Stabilizers were spreading out and bolts were being driven into the concrete. Nestor chuckled. "Until we're sure about all this, let's prepare to stay." She looked at Elvox again. "Loytnant, unless you wish to risk life and limb, I suggest you remain here as our guest. I hope that won't be too inconvenient."

The winds outside were already rising above a hundred kilometers an hour. He shook his head in resignation. "I'll have to send a message to my lander."

"Feel free," Nestor said, pointing out the communications panel.

Within the hour all three ships were firmly rooted into the concrete. The winds began to show their true faces. By early evening the cloud cover was clear and stars twinkled in the oncoming night. Minutes later a vast wet front swept over and dropped a flood on the plains of concrete.

Most of Nestor's entourage were preparing to sleep in the cargo bay. Spare sleeping pads and blankets were being brought out, and hot drinks were served. Two women came up to the bridge to talk with Nestor, carrying ampoules of liquid for all of them.

Elvox watched Nestor closely. The women were musicians from her entourage, and their manner with her was informal, relaxed. The way her lander crew acted, the whole affair might have been a family outing. Elvox wondered how she kept discipline. But it wasn't his concern. The drink was relaxing him, but he couldn't shake a kind of awe at being in Nestor's presence.

Some of her women were very attractive. He hadn't seen so many women in one place for a month or more. The USC ship in orbit was crewed by both men and women, but on this mission the proportions had been hastily mixed, and before that, Elvox had served on an all-male ship. Most of the women on the main ship were married or career-minded. Here, things seemed much looser. Not that he was a Lothario under any circumstances. Still the old, familiar pressures were building, and he tried to push them aside. The drink wasn't helping.

It hardly seemed possible for Nestor to be scheming all the time. Perhaps she was letting her guard down. He decided to play along, make the best of an awkward situation. If Nestor was offering her hospitality out of some ulterior motive, perhaps he could turn the tables on her. It wouldn't be an unpleasant job.

While Kawashita talked with the pilot, Nestor took Elvox aside. "I've given up my own cabin," she said. "I'll be sleeping in a small cubicle usually reserved for Kiril." She indicated the pilot. "He'll sleep on the bridge. I don't recommend you sleep in the cargo bay. My friends are always on the lookout for fresh provisions. I doubt you'd get any sleep."

"Doesn't sound too unpleasant," Elvox said.

"Yes, but you don't know my crew. Beyond that, space is pretty limited. I'm giving Yoshio complete privacy for a while, and as you can see, there's not much room here for more than one."

"I can sleep in a corridor," Elvox suggested. Was she joking with him, about the crew? He had heard stories—

"The best idea might be for you to share my cubicle. There's room enough for two, and I don't want to be accused of shirking my social obligations to United Stars."

He felt as if he were dreaming. Nestor and her family were celebrities, to say the least. Some maintained they were sacred monsters, necessary in society but hardly respectable. Still, she seemed reasonably decent. She was also attractive when not bent on business. The totality was not undesirable. He didn't know what to say, however, so he just nodded.

"Good," Nestor said. "This'll give Yoshio a chance to get used to the modern facilities."

The utilities on her lander were fancier than those on the main USC ship. Kawashita, considering his position and status, would probably never have to make do with less. Elvox watched Nestor from behind as she gave her pilot instructions for the morning.

Outside, the storm was letting loose with alarming fury.

"What held it all back so long?" Nestor asked. Elvox tried to get a view through a rain- and slush-spattered port.

"Landers aren't made to withstand hurricanes," the pilot said.

"Maybe they were just being humanitarians," Elvox suggested. "They just wanted Yoshio rescued."

"That doesn't answer my question. *What* did they leave behind that controlled this until we landed? Is there a weather machine someplace? Or were we just lucky to be in time for the waterworks?"

They were almost shouting to overcome the noise outside. "We can investigate when things clear up," Elvox said. "Right now, I'm a little afraid to go to sleep."

"It's my job to worry about it," the pilot said.

"Kiril, don't forget Loytnant Elvox is a lander captain, too," Nestor said.

"Of course. But I think our ships are tough enough. Everybody go to sleep. I'll yell if we get blown apart."

"Very reassuring," Kawashita said. He looked up from a technical manual on the lander's primary operating systems. His tapas was busily translating from a queue of definition requests, and his eyes were squinty. "I know nothing about weather. I was never outside dome until now."

"To rest with all of us," Nestor said. "Yoshio, you know the way to your cabin. Mr. Elvox, are you happy with the sleeping arrangements?"

"Yes." Happy was not quite the word. Uncertain, perhaps.

"Good. You'll find the cabin just around the curve clockwise from Yoshio's quarters. I'll be down in a while."

Elvox walked with the Japanese. He was curious about the man's story, but discretion was best for the moment. It was a credit to Nestor and her people that the man was accepting things so calmly. Kawashita gestured for Elvox to wait as they came to his door.

"I am not familiar with some things here," he said. "It would embarrass to ask *her* about them. Could you explain?"

"I can try," Elvox said. "What don't you understand?"

"The bed. I was shown, but it is not easy."

"Of course." The sleep field was easy to operate but difficult to explain. He showed Kawashita how to lie across it for maximum comfort, and how to set the timer for a gentle let-down after however many hours he wished to sleep.

"And these?" Kawashita pointed to the sleep-induction phones.

"Try them on," Elvox suggested. "Over your ears, just like old-fashioned . . . like the ones in your time."

Kawashita put them on and Elvox adjusted the knob for mild relaxation. Kawashita's eyes began to droop, and his face relaxed. Suddenly he tensed and removed the phones, handing them back to Elvox. "Don't need that now," he said. "Sleep enough without."

"They're not the most pleasant way to sleep. But you do wake up feeling you've slept a whole night, when only a half hour has passed. They're useful for long watches."

"Yes, I see that," Kawashita said. "I was a pilot. There were many days I could not sleep, thinking about the battle, flying. This would have been good. But not now." He walked across the cabin. "The lavatory bothers me very much. Have questions—" He cut himself short and smiled politely, then shook his head. "No, never mind. I will ask later. I thank, and ask you forgive me very much."

"No forgiveness for asking questions," Elvox said. Kawashita's face fell. "I mean, questions are essential. We expect them and don't mind at all."

He still looked worried when Elvox left. Before the door closed, Elvox heard him muttering.

"He's been doing that a lot," Nestor said behind Elvox. He turned in surprise.

"Oh?"

"It's not the most polite thing to do, but we've been tapping and listening."

"I see."

Nestor held up a translator tapas. "He's talking to someone named Ko. Every chance, he discusses Japanese history with Ko. I suspect it's been going on for some time, since they—he—makes reference to different events across about a thousand years. Right now," she indicated the tapas screen, "they're talking about the Japanese invasion of Manchuria, the Chinese incident, and the destruction of an Earth city called Nanking. In detail. Assigning blame to individuals."

"Why?"

"We don't know. We don't know whether this Ko ever existed."

"Perfidisian, perhaps?" Elvox said.

"No. There doesn't seem to be anything in the cabin with him. Ko, whatever he or it was, is purely imaginary now."

"But why the debate?"

Nestor shook her head. "Go ahead to the cabin, Mr. Elvox. I'll be with you shortly."

There was only one sleep-field in the cubicle he and Nestor were sharing. He wondered if he should use it, and decided it was more polite to take out the secondary mattress and lie on that. With the lights out, and the ship shuddering, he felt an odd smugness, something he hadn't known in years.

He was almost asleep when Nestor entered the cabin. She left the light off and removed her clothes in the glow from the corridor. Then she bent over Elvox. "Loytnant," she said, "unless it violates your creed, I'd much rather have something warmer than just a sleep field."

"I—" He hesitated, knowing his barriers were down, and not particularly caring. "So would I."

"Thank you, Mr. Elvox." She fitted herself against his back and put her arms around him. "You're a gentleman and a scholar."

SIX

It was a terrible time. Alae marched back and forth in their cabin, screaming at Oomalo—though he knew very well she was only screaming in his direction—and twirling a piece of bedding like a banner.

"Why should we have given up? There's nothing here, and if there is, *he* has it—a damned savage! What do we end up with? Nothing!"

"Our job was over anyway," Oomalo said softly. "When the signals stopped. We don't need any more money. Our employers could care less where we are or what we're doing now that the job is over. They might relocate us if we make up another contract—and that isn't likely. But it all amounts to the same thing." The disappointment hadn't hit him as deeply, but resentment still gnawed at him. "It isn't all over yet," he said, aware he was contradicting himself. "We may still have a claim. We have to wait until the Centrum ship arrives."

"I'd rather leave now before we go through any more humiliation."

Oomalo shrugged. "We're bolted down and we can't leave until the storm passes. I suggest you relax and—"

"It was peaceful out there," she said. "With the routine, the jobs that always needed doing, and no way we could ever lose our home or get into trouble. It was secure. We traded that for this. For concrete and emptiness and a foul little man who wouldn't even tell us where he came from!" She flung the sheet away and sat hard on the sleep-field frame. "We should have killed him. Hidden him or broken him down in the lander waste units. We're just not ruthless enough."

Oomalo nodded and sat across from her on a pile of bedclothes. "We didn't do it, and now it's too late. It just takes patience from here in . . ."

Alae lay back and stared at the overhead blankly, her gray eyes wide. "Toys," she said. "Baubles. The most dangerous things imaginable. Passion and need." She straightened up. "How long has it been since we conjoined?"

"I don't know."

"Years. Even that passion had left us."

He lifted up his hands and shook his head. "It was no longer needed."

"It was a poison. But you know that it's returned? Don't you feel it? It's come back to add to the misery."

He wasn't sure he felt anything. Alae's femininity had never been very strong, and in time he had simply blanked out the fact that they were man and wife. They were companions above and beyond anything else.

"I even need *that* now," she said.

Oomalo took a deep breath, put his hands down to lift himself off the bedclothes, and hesitated. Alae looked at him almost fiercely. She untied her robe.

The ship vibrated in the wind, and a weird whistling noise made Oomalo open his eyes. Alae was breathing through her teeth as she rode him. Abruptly he sat up and held her around the ribs, squeezing with all his strength. She exploded a breath and struggled to take in another. He didn't let her. "Damn you," she grunted. "Let me breathe." He rolled her over and pinned her against the yielding sleep-field with an arm across her neck.

"Are you done with the histrionics?" he asked. Her eyes widened and she groaned, twisting her hips against him. "Are you done?"

"No," she wheezed.

He pulled his arm up and felt the anger getting stronger in him. He didn't know who or what he was trying to hurt. With typical restraint he didn't hit her hard. For both of them it seemed to work. She screwed her face up and screamed into his breast. He felt nothing as he came in her, but his tension subsided.

Outside, the rain increased and the wind drove drops of water and ice against the hull like a crowd's fists.

_____

SEVEN

When Kawashita awoke, the storm was still raging. He lay
in the sleepfield, listening to the muffled noises of the
wind, the rain, acclimating himself to the surroundings.
Each morning he awoke, he had to swallow back a
nameless fear—that it was all still illusion, that he was still
in the dome. He sat up, rubbed his face with his hands,
and went into the lavatory. Ignoring the strange devices,
he washed his face off with a thin stream of water and
held his hands out, examining the fingernails. How often
—in how many different situations—had he gone through
just such a ritual? It seemed to be a connection, a common
thread through all of his lives. He felt ready to talk to Ko
again.

"Ko!" he called. There was no answer. "Come, we
haven't finished yet. Many years yet." He looked around
the cabin, frowning. "Ko?" The panic arose again. Ko had
stayed with him when all the others had left. Was he to be
deserted again, left in a strange, empty ship, with Ko
gone, and all the others, too? He sucked in his breath and
tried to bury his fear, concentrating on the strength in his
stomach. He reached down to feel his testicles. They were
tight, drawn-up. Centuries ago, lifetimes ago, he had been
told that was a sign of impending panic and disgrace. He
pulled the testicles down as best he could, and his fear
seemed to subside.

The fact that Ko was gone did not necessarily mean the
others were gone. He groped for a way to that foggy reali-
zation—to understanding the difference between Ko and
the ones who had found him. Perhaps Ko . . .

He had been brave so long, had witnessed the
strangeness and newness. It would do no good to examine
things too closely before he was ready. What he and Ko

had been doing had helped, for there was blame to be established, but perhaps they had been on the wrong track.

He exercised briefly, regulating his breath to calm himself. Then he dressed and opened the door. He remembered his way around the ship well enough.

When the others awoke, Kawashita was in the lounge ahead of them, eating from a plate of what looked like partially cooked vegetables. He had learned how to customize the menu's offerings. The machinery presented few problems to him—he was a quick learner, always had been—but the people . . . he was not used to so many people.

Without Ko, he would have to pursue another tack. He made his decision.

"Good morning, Yoshio," Anna said.

He stood and bowed quickly to Nestor and the man called Elvox. "Good morning, if it is morning."

"For us, close enough," Anna said.

"I am ready to tell my story."

"Fine. I'll get my first officer and an unabridged tapas bank." She left and returned a few minutes later with the woman, who carried a suitcase-like object and two tapas pads. She was about seventy, though she looked younger. Anna had explained juvenates to Yoshio, and he understood their effects fairly well. The first officer sat down beside Yoshio and smiled at him.

"My name is Carina," she said, arranging her equipment. Anna and Elvox sat together on the opposite side of the table.

"I am honored," Yoshio said, standing and bowing, then bowing to the others. He sat again, folding his hands on the table top. "If you are ready . . ."

"We are," Carina said.

"I was born in the twentieth century," Yoshio began, "thirteen years after my nation's victory over the Russians at Tsushima."

"That was 1905," Carina said, "so you were born in 1918."

"Yes. I joined the armed forces in 1940 and became a flier. I flew in airplanes launched from large, flat-topped ships called aircraft carriers. I was a part of *Kido Butai*, the carrier strike force of Japan. I was an enlisted pilot, not very experienced at first, and I did not take part in the

early battles with the United States of America—in the attack at Pearl Harbor, or the Philippines. I flew my first
missions in the Coral Sea, near Australia, and was proud
to shoot down three aircraft, and help sink the Lexington
aircraft carrier. We also thought we sank Yorktown, another carrier, but not so. My airplanes were Aichi type
99s, what the Americans called Vals. I was a gunner usually, seated behind the pilot, but I had done much flying
alone in trainers and fighters a few times.

"My air group was assigned to the carrier *Hiryu*. I flew
a type 99 to capture the small American-occupied island
on Midway. This was in the middle of 1942. Many things
escape my memory, so if I am inaccurate, tell me . . ."

"Why tell us the story now, Yoshio?" Anna asked.

"Hht!" He drew in his breath, stood, and bowed. "Many
pardon. You are not ready."

"No, no!" Carina said, giving Anna a withering glance.
"We're ready. Anna means, are you sure you're ready to
tell us? We are most interested in your welfare."

"I am ready. Appreciate your thoughts. I will go on."
He sat down. "We lost many ships in that battle. I was let
to read how many, but that was long ago. Have not paid
much attention to numbers since."

"Who let you read?" Elvox asked.

"Those who capture me. I never saw them, I think. I
tell you how. Island was attacked early in the morning,
about six. I flew in the first wave of planes, led by Lieutenant Joichi Tomonoga. Before we fly, we eat victory
breakfast—rice, soybean soup, chestnuts and sake. We
leave at twenty minutes after four—I am looking at a Rolex watch my father gave me." He pointed at his bare
wrist, his eyes intense. "Later, lost the watch at sea. I
climbed in the back of my dive bomber. It is going to be
glorious. My pilot has scarf around his head, and belt of a
thousand stitches is wrapped around my waist under the
flight suit. My mother stood on street corner, asking pas-
sers-by to add stitch, until all prayers and wishes go with
me, a thousand.

"There is not much resistance. American pilots from
Midway fly twenty, twenty-five fighters to attack, but our
Zeros engage. They shoot down clumsy old planes, called
Buffalos, and new fighters not yet proved, Wildcats I
think. Twenty-two shot down!" He spread his hands out.

"We feel like just having done *kampai*—like long bout with *sake*. Then we bomb Midway, two islands, Eastern and Sand. A companion flies around Sand Island and drops his bomb on a storage tank for oil. It looks like whole island is carried away in the explosion. Eastern Island looks very bad, too, but our commander calls for a second attack. This is about seven o'clock, and we feel upset that second wave might be needed to finish our work. But we return to *Hiryu*, refuel, and load more bombs in case we are needed in a third or fourth attack. This is between eight and ten o'clock." He tapped his wrist again.

"We are told that Americans have attacked our carriers, are still attacking, but the bombs miss, the torpedos are awful, our ships just swerve around them. And the Americans die, whole squadrons. Very brave. But when we land, there is much confusion on our decks—planes being brought up and down elevators, being loaded with bombs, then the bombs removed and replaced by torpedos, because we do not know just where American planes are coming from, and whether we must attack Midway, or carriers, or both. This confusion goes on and stories are everywhere—that we have sunk American carriers, that some of our ships are damaged. We don't know what to believe." He smiled apologetically.

"It is decided, after more than eighty American planes have been shot down, that if aircraft carriers are nearby, they have been exhausted. So we re-arm planes with bombs. At ten fifteen, another attack—but from where? Twelve torpedo bombers. Three get through to our ships and are brought down by guns, two escape. Seven are shot down by our fighters. Very brave. Our carrier is separated from the others, under cloud cover, very fortunate. We hear sounds of more attacks across ocean, see bomb sprays, smoke, fire. At noon, I fly with another strike. We are looking for the American carrier—but which one? It cannot be *Yorktown*, she was sunk or badly damaged at Coral Sea—"

"Just a moment," Carina interrupted, looking over her tapas screen. "The Japanese lost three carriers by ten-thirty—*Akagi, Kaga, Soryu*. They were all burning badly by that time. The *Hiryu* was the only one left functioning."

Kawashita nodded. "Yes. But we did not know this for

sure, not on the flight deck. We learned in the air, and some of us did not believe. I didn't. How could it have happened? Rear Admiral Yamaguchi orders us to attack the American carrier or carriers, and just an hour later, we find *Yorktown*. She has been fixed in just days—a job that should have taken months. What power the Americans have! This is very frightening. But what they had brought back by miracle, we can sink all the same. Our flight leader, Michio Kobayashi this time, gives us courage. Our courage is in the center of our being, in our stomachs, he tells us. But our luck is not good this time. We are attacked by American fighters and lose five or six planes immediately. We approach the American carrier flying in a formation of V's—" he held his hands up with palms together, fingers apart, and spaced several gestures in a bigger V—"and attacked from the port side, at an angle of seventy-two degrees. Two more planes are shot down, one Kobayashi's. I watch his plane fall apart and hit the ocean. Helpless, just shooting at American fighters, not knowing when we will go down like Kobayashi.

"I remember one thing. I think it was before we bombed the *Yorktown*. An American fighter pulls up behind our plane, very close, not firing. I think he is out of ammunition. He swings back and forth, and I follow him with my gun, trying to guess where he will go so I can fire into him. Then he comes very close, almost touching our tail with his propellor. But he decides not to and flies away. I see his face. I see his anger. It is the first time I have seen an American close-up since I was a young child. It frightens me. He looks very brave and fierce, like he is about to destroy his plane and ours, just for vengeance. I think I just look scared.

"We drop our bombs and start to pull away. I see one bomb heading for the carrier, and one landing in the water near it. The explosion in the water tilts the ship, and the second bomb strikes it. Another bomb flies right down the stack. Three hits! For a while we fly around the carrier, firing our guns. Two more planes are shot down. I remember watching men throw burning trash off the fantail, all like in a dream. Boxes of wood and other trash float behind the carrier.

"We have only five planes left, so we return to the *Hiryu* and land, very tired. We eat. Lieutenant Tomonoga takes off with five planes to make sure the *Yorktown* is out of action. But we are not able to finish our meal before we are attacked again. I run to the plane and meet my pilot, who does not smile or say anything. We are all deadly tired. We take off to defend our ship. The Aichi Type 99 will not be very good against the American fighters, we know, but it is better to be in the air rather than on deck as a target.

"We do not stop all the planes. Several bombs hit the forward flight deck. The forward elevator is blown up against the bridge, like a can lid pried by a giant's hand. We know that we cannot land now. We have fought fiercely, and have lost everything. It is best to die fighting. So we try to pursue the Americans. My pilot is shot in the arm and across the neck. I talk to him, but he is losing consciousness. The plane flies for some distance, going lower, waves striking wings, and we are down. The nose crushes him, comes up with the impact, and I am thrown through the back, crack my ribs on the canopy. I climb off the tail as fast as I can, for the plane will go down like a rock. It is painful to swim, but I have to, or the plane will suck me down with it. Then, in my life vest, I tread water and wait for the battle to be over.

"It is early evening when I see that the *Hiryu* has come close to me. She is now dead in the water, listing to the port side. Destroyers—the *Kazagumo* and *Makigumo*—are taking away her crew. She is being abandoned. I swim toward her, shouting as loud as I can, but no one hears me. The ship is groaning, belching steam, metal screaming louder than I can. The destroyers leave, sailing away from me. I see men still on the carrier's flight deck, waving at the other ships. They may be on board to scuttle the ship, or perhaps the destroyers could hold no more. But after a while they walk out of my line of sight.

"In the twilight, I climb up a gangway hanging from the side. It takes me half an hour to reach the hangar deck. There is no one. I feel very alone.

"It is dark before I am well enough to walk around. I find an electric lantern and go to a battle dressing station on the hangar deck, coughing in the smoke. I take a first-aid kit into the open air on a gun mount and bandage my side. There are bodies near the gun. They have no heads.

"I wander over the ship for an hour, looking for the

men I have seen. There are explosions from below, and I hear screams, but I don't know if they are men or metal. In the officer's mess I find food, changing lanterns after my first wears out. Then I go to the bridge. I hear two men speaking, and it frightens me—perhaps they are ghosts. But I recognize one voice. It is Captain Tomeo Kaku. The other has to be Admiral Tamon Yamaguchi. I shine my light into the bridge and see they are strapped to the helm, talking, waiting for the ship to go down. When they see me, Yamaguchi asks who I am. I say I am a pilot.

" 'The pilots did well today,' he says. 'It is an honorable fight, and we have sunk many American carriers, many ships. They will never recover from this.' He said it would be best, since the ship wasn't sinking fast enough, that we all go below and commit *seppuku*. But I am not willing to die. 'I will fight again for the emperor,' I tell him. He becomes angry, but the Captain talks to him, reasons. I am young, able to fight again. So I help them untie themselves, then leave and go down to my bunkroom. I search for things I want to take with me when I leave. My Rolex is gone, ripped off in the crash, so I take an alarm clock. I find boxes in the corridor filled with tinned fish, and a storage locker with bottles of medicinal brandy and some *sake*. I load these into a canvas bag tied to a rope, which I swing out over the side. It will wait for me at the water line. I have to find a raft fast, then, because the ship is listing more and the bag will soon be underwater. A raft hangs from a single cord tied to a girder, so I cut it loose and drop it into the water near the gangway. I climb down, more rapidly this time, and put my finds into the raft. Then I push away from the *Hiryu* with an oar.

"In the early morning, after I have slept for some hours, I hear a tremendous roar, and I see the dawn sky light up with blasts. I wait for day, but the carrier is gone. She has been scuttled. There are no planes in the sky, no one to rescue me. A few stars are still out.

"Then I see something I cannot explain. It is a bright spot in the sky, like a star but moving. It winks and goes out, just as a plane will wink when it is flying in sunlight and turns to flash its wings. Perhaps it is a plane, very high, I think.

"But then it comes back, much larger, the size of my

thumbnail. It is completely silent. It swoops down to where oil from the Hiryu is still bubbling, and I see it is very large—perhaps twice the length of the carrier. It is a flattened ball, with glowing tear-drops sticking from its sides. When it flies toward me, the water around the raft begins to steam. I look up and see myself mirrored in the bottom of the thing, all the world reflected from horizon to horizon. I know we in Japan have no aircraft like that, and I think perhaps this is what really sank the *Akagi, Kaga, Soryu.* And I am not afraid any more.

"I know I am going to die."

EIGHT

Kawashita held his breath for a moment, then smiled and drank half a glass of beer. "I feel odd then, like electricity is going through me." He looked around the cabin. "Pardon. I have been talking about your people, about the war, and I do not know what you think. It is very hard—what we did—"

"We aren't Americans, Yoshio," Anna said softly. "It was a long time ago, things have changed."

"*Desu-ka*? Yes, of course. I continue. I find I am not in my raft. For a long time I am examined by things—metal tools, buzzing machines. I lie on a metal bench with a soft part in the middle. I am naked. Twenty meters away, perhaps, in the dark, there is a circle, and in the circle a face. No mouth, no nose, just wide black eyes. I also see one arm—could be an arm—with a hand. Nothing holds me down, so I stand, walk into dark, stop by the lighted circle. There is nothing behind it—it floats in air—but face and arm are full, like in three dimensions. Nothing moves. I turn away and see the bench is gone. Another circle is in its place, with what looks like bird—but not a bird. A man with a sharp, beaked face and thin fur or feathers all over him, with large, naked ears. I see four circles, back and forth across the dark place, before I feel floor going away. I think I sleep."

"Sounds like you were shown a Minkie and a Crocerian," Elvox said. "What did the others look like?"

"Not sure. Uglier—one like fish that sucks on other fish—what do you call it?"

"Lampreys," Carina said.

"But with snake body and limbs . . . reversed." He demonstrated by trying to bend his arms backward at the elbow.

"That could be an Aighor," Elvox said. "It's obvious they didn't show you what they looked like themselves."

"I do not know. I believe I never saw them, never saw anything truly *from* them. But may have seen and not recognized. When I awake, I am in a house like my grandparents' house near Yokosuka. There is a forest around it. I can walk as far as I want, in any direction, but I know it is not for real. The house was burned in nineteen thirty-five. And the forest cleared for lumber. For a long time, I think I am dreaming. Then people appear, mostly women, but now—how to say—personable? Most cooperative, like in a pillow-book, but not real. I think perhaps my baser instincts will be provided for by captors."

"The women change, however, and soon will not do everything I want. Before long, a whole village grows up around me, a building added each night when I sleep. I am not dreaming. I am making things appear. I decide captors, whoever they are, have the power to let me create whatever is in my mind. They must be *kami*—divine spirits. Very divine spirits. So I worship them. I build a small shrine and put one part aside for my ancestral *kami*, one part for these new inhuman *kami*, new powers.

"Each day I walk farther. Finally I leave the forest and come to a city, very much like Yokohama. Thousands of people live in it. I am proud to be able to think of so much, but I don't take advantage of it. I try to find recruiters so I can go back to my ship, to the war. Perhaps I am really home, I think—hope against hope. But there are no ships, no war. Just city. I cannot redeem myself for cowardice. I cannot sacrifice myself for my emperor. I am truly captured, not just insane. I decide to create other things, and find my limitations.

"In morning, I squat in my shrine—I have built another in the city—and concentrate on as much of Japan as I can. Then I take a train and go away from the city, which is very much like Yokohama, to Kyoto. And there I live, work, marry. Have a child. But nobody grows old. I help design airplanes in a factory—airplanes nobody uses, probably—waiting for war to come and find me. I feel that none of my workers or friends change, become more worthy. Everyone stays the same. Soon I am bored. I think of other things—about heroic times, when there were ways to gain honor and live a full life. I think of days after

Japan was created, and of the Sun hiding in a cave, and what happened to Her. I think of Jemmu Tenno. But nothing changes outside—it is just very deep night. I don't know enough about such things.

"So I think of a library. It is barely clear in my mind before I am wandering through stacks of books and racks of newspapers, reading about all sorts of things. I learn what has happened since I left. I find news about the war. Real news? I don't know. But there is so much, so self-consistent, that I decide I cannot have made it all up. My captors must inject some of real world into my creation. I find English books about the war, and other subjects, so I learn how to read and speak English. I don't need to rest, so I study for days, weeks, time no matter. I learn the war had gone badly. We had lost. And surrendered. The emperor declared that the beginning of Japan was a myth, and he was not descended from the Sun Goddess, but was a mortal."

"Emperor Showa," Carina interjected.

"Yes, Hirohito when he was alive. That night, to soothe myself, I hang a ribbon for Japan in my shrine. Then I go to other parts of the library and find books on Japanese history, besides traditional ones I have read in school. My thoughts about the past are clearing. I decide first on nineteenth century, since I had heard a lot about it from my grandfather, who was actual samurai. I learn about *Bushido*, the warrior's way. Next morning, I go outside library, and nineteenth century is outside door. I go out to live as a traveling priest. That lasts, I think, for many decades.

"But after turn of century, as war with Russia grows near, I become unhappy. I go to shrine and make it night outside. With that night goes two wives, one who had died in childbirth, three children, many friends.

"When day comes, I am in a Japan I have never seen before. I haven't created it myself, not intentionally. I decide it has been created for me by the *kami*.

"It is the twelfth century. I am a man named Tokimasa, a very important adviser. I begin to see what the *kami* wish me to do. I am to examine Japanese history, to find what has flawed us."

"They told you that?" Elvox asked.

"No, never speak. Never show. But this is strong suggestion, no? I think perhaps I will see how to change history, to bring Japan to enlightenment before my time comes—an experiment. To decrease pain and killing and ignorance. I try to . . ."

He stopped and looked down at the table. "That is all my shame. From the very beginning it is my shame, to be captured alive, to accept the destruction of my land, to act so before the *kami* who are testing me. You say there are things I will have trouble understanding. Well, you cannot easily understand my shame."

"Hoji Tokimasa was a member of the Taira clan," Carina said. "He was given charge of two Minamoto boys, Yoritomo and Yoshitsune, sons of Kiyomori, a chieftan killed by the Taira. Yoritomo married your daughter . . . uh, Masa, but you didn't accept the marriage until they had a child. When Yoritomo staged a revolt against the Taira, you . . . uh, Tokimasa switched allegiance."

"That is history," Kawashita said. "And I was too weak to change it second time around. When I created, what I meddled with—it would have been better if I had killed Masa in her bed as an infant." His voice was quavering with bitterness, and his eyes brimmed with tears.

Elvox was impatient. "How long before the Perfidisians left and everything stopped?"

"I don't know. I try to change things, but everything snaps back. I try to run away by making another world, but I have to return. Time does not mean much under the dome. The last years, I advise Yoritomo after he makes himself the first universal *shogun*—the first to establish the place of the *shoguns* in Japan."

"When did the trouble begin?" Anna asked.

Kawashita shook his head. "It was awful."

"Storm's letting up," the pilot observed, entering the lounge. "Anna, we have a signal from the *Peloros*. Two Centrum ships have entered orbit. They're waiting for permission to send down landers."

Anna looked across the table at Kawashita. "Well?"

"Yes?"

"You seem to be provisional owner. Can they land?"

"Of course."

The pilot handed a tapas insert to Elvox. "And here's a message from the two men you sent into the dome."

"Yes. I have some questions about that. Yoshio, we measured that dome. It couldn't possibly hold everything you've told us about. How do you explain that?"

"I do not know." He bowed to them. "I will go rest now. Is it possible—" He paused, his eyebrows coming together and his lips working. "Is it possible to destroy the dome and everything under it?"

"I wouldn't advise that," Anna said. "Go rest now and we'll talk about it later." Kawashita nodded sharply and left the lounge.

"Looks like you're mother to the oldest child in the world," Elvox said.

Nestor shook her head. "He's had a rough time," she said, hugging the loytnant's arm. "Have to wait until we hear the rest of the story, right? Patience. If I've learned anything, it's to let times like these unfold at their own pace. I'd pay attention to the Waunters now, frankly. But what about your investigations? Can we share and share alike?"

Elvox looked at the tapas insert, then nodded. "I don't see why not. You can investigate as easily as we." He took a tapas from Carina, programmed the decode sequence, and held the machine out for them to watch.

When it was done, they leaned back in their seats and Elvox sighed. "I apologize if my men think it's haunted."

"It's understandable," Carina said. "Two hundred bodies, half looking like they've just fallen in their tracks, and the rest slaughtered, throats cut, limbs scattered."

"How could it happen?" Elvox asked. "Who would want to go around killing androids?"

"Maybe they killed each other," Anna said. "Maybe they thought they were real, and held real grudges."

"It doesn't seem to have been one big battle," Carina said. "They seem to have attacked each other at random. No sides chosen, no special uniforms, no banners. Just streets filled with bodies. What did Yoshio have to do with it?"

Elvox put his hand on the pad. "I think the Perfidisians left just when the slaughter was getting good. They kept the basic environment for him but cut back on the androids, the scenery, most of the illusion. So the androids fell in the middle of a pitched battle, whatever sort of battle it was."

"They left him because he started a ruckus?" Carina said, incredulous.

Anna shook her head. "I don't pretend to understand Perfidisians, but they must have left for better reasons than that. A scientist just doesn't leave his lab because the rats squabble. But think what Kawashita must have gone through. All of a sudden, his dream was over. He was surrounded by bodies. Who knows? They might have been friends, fellow soldiers, wives, nobles. Hell, he was there long enough to have had children and grandchildren. Suddenly they all died, stopped functioning. Well, because of the battle, maybe it seemed like a punishment from God—from the *kami*. Maybe he went crazy for a while, still lived with phantoms."

"And the Waunters found him that way," Elvox said. "But if they had him living whole lives in the dome, they had to provide more than is there now. The roads just end at the walkway around the perimeter. Some buildings are cut in half. Whole forests are bisected, and that doesn't make for a credible world. Something had to keep the cage out of his view."

"What?" Anna asked.

"I have an idea," Kiril said. "It's a little hard to conceive. Maybe he really did have a whole world at his disposal. Whenever he headed for the walkway, for the cage wall, everything changed behind him, and he was somehow turned around to head back toward the center of the dome. To him, it would have seemed like one long walk."

"He wouldn't have just lived in one restricted section, then," Elvox said.

"He already told us about that," Anna said. "He had all of Japan to travel in. But where is the dome now? I mean, what locale is set up inside?"

"Perhaps Heian-Kyô, or Kamakura," Carina said. "He was dressed like a samurai, but he could have put on the armor when the illusions stopped. He was probably scared out of his wits."

"That much seems certain," Anna said. She looked at Elvox. "Do you have a few hours before you have to go back?"

"If I leave a message." He removed the tapas insert

from the pad. "I assume my men delivered this after sending it on from the lander."

"If you trained them right. I'd enjoy your company here. Place your message?"

He agreed. In the lift, he stood behind her, frowning. Until now, he hadn't violated any of the codes of a United Stars Officer. He had been completely loyal and dedicated. Was he compromising his duty by staying with Nestor? He didn't think he was. On the whole, they would both benefit by not being evasive or hiding information.

Nestor took care of Kawashita honorably and without apparent guile. She could afford to—she wasn't desperate. But then, neither was United Stars. As the largest human consolidation, USC had its hand in thousands of similar enterprises. How could he decide without bias? She was a persuasive woman. And was that persuasiveness deliberate? Or perhaps even worse, it was possible that her actions—while not deliberate—were part of the unconscious matrix of behaviors which made her what she was, Anna Sigrid Nestor. Her instincts could be far more dangerous than any subterfuge.

"I feel a little guilty," he said as they entered their cabin.

"Why?" she asked.

"This may not be in the line of duty."

"It may not be for me, either. So we are both consorting with the enemy."

"No, not exactly, but—" He laughed.

"My people will get as much out of this as yours, everyone will be happy. So far, it looks a lot like a farce."

"How's that?" He thought she meant their own behavior, and he stiffened.

"This whole affair. An empty planet, heavily explored and charted—for nothing. Blank slate."

"Oh."

"Don't worry. Everything will turn out fine. What would you be doing in your lander now?"

"Filing reports."

"We've already sent an unedited transcript of Yoshio's talk to your ship in orbit. What else could you report about?"

"Nothing my crew can't handle," Elvox admitted.

NINE

If most people could be compared to dull glows, Nestor was white heat. Her eyes were wide and full of energy even while her voice was measured and restrained. She never said a thing that hadn't been passed through a dozen self-contained censors. But she had ways of letting out her energy. One was in a sleepfield.

She was almost too much for him. On his home world, such cooperation and enthusiasm would have been unseemly. He was almost afraid of her independence, of having to satisfy both of them. Yet she didn't demand more than he could give. All in all, they matched each other rather well.

After they'd made love, he sat up in the sleepfield and folded his hands on his stomach. "I was raised on a pretty straight-laced world," he said.

"So was I—though my world was a ship."

"No, I mean where love is concerned."

"You've had some good teachers, wherever you came from," she said, smiling at him sleepily.

He stroked her shoulder and reached down to caress her breast. Her skin was soft, just taking on the matte texture that shows a woman is leaving girlhood behind. He found it much more attractive than the plastic tightness that usually brought approval.

"This means a great deal to me," he ventured. "Where I come from, we believe in commitments."

"Mm," she breathed, snuggling against him.

"I know it's a release . . . shared release of tensions." His words sounded incredibly inept to him. "And I don't think you're trying to win me over."

"Already have," she said under his arm.

He shook his head and said no more.

The Centrum team visited Nestor's lander the next day.

Four men and six women *ex officio* judges took the case under consideration after listening to the depositions. Half of the proceedings were held aboard the USC lander, and a tour of the Waunter vehicle was made as well. The Waunters watched without expression, grimly confident—it seemed to Elvox—that they had no case at all. True enough, the Centrum was seldom called in to intervene on the behalf of individuals, dealing instead with entities like USC or Nestor's far-flung operation.

The Waunters could not give up all hope, however. Alae prepared a deposition on her own, using what legal advice she could glean out of the lander's library. The Centrum took it under advisement.

Nestor—in the presence of the judges—behaved according to strict protocol. Elvox was an officer attached to United Stars, she was a representative of separate interests. They were cordial but aloof.

The next evening, however, he was again a friend and confidant. They ate a late snack and made love. Before sleep, he realized how beautiful she really was. He had thought of her as moderately attractive before, but when she laughed, she went right over the line into beauty. It was like watching a monument turn into a living woman.

As they ate breakfast in the lounge—alone, as if by assumption of the crew and Kawashita—he felt a moment of emotional vertigo. It was worse now. Not only did he not care about duty, he hardly cared about returning to United Stars. He chastised himself for thinking like an adolescent.

"I've been working for USC for seven years," he said.

"They must have gotten you young."

"Nineteen. How does that stack up against your crew, in terms of experience?"

She shrugged. "Depends on what you're an expert at."

"General ship work, I suppose. Command of equipment watches, sortie captain."

She cocked her head and looked at him. "Julio, you're not thinking of transferring, are you?"

He didn't know how to answer. "It crossed my mind," he said finally. "I've been comparing services. Your crew—"

"Works very hard," she threw in.

"Yes, but the work seems much more basic, important. In the action."

"We're both here. USC can't be that far away from the good stuff."

"And besides," he said, "you're here." He chuckled knowingly but watched her expression.

"Close to the action, as it were," she joked, eyes twinkling.

"Yes."

"Indeed I am. Some of my crew never see me for weeks at a stretch."

He felt like a fish being played on a line. Her words were double-edged. "I always honor my commitments," he said.

"Yes, I would think that."

"But a lateral transfer, with warning, is allowed in our contracts."

"I could offer you a post," Anna said. "The work's hard, but . . . I think you'd fit in."

He grinned broadly, caught himself, and felt his face flush. She laughed and patted him on the shoulder. "But I'm in command, and I'm not always reasonable. Sometimes I do monstrous, foul things—and make my officers drop years off their lifespans, right and left, like dandruff. You don't believe that, do you?" she asked, this time with a bite in her tone.

"I believe you can be tough," Elvox said.

"Tough is not the word," she said, looking away from him. Something seemed to cloud her expression. "We'll think about it."

In the days following, he realized that there were competent people, and there were masters. Nestor was a master at what she did. She wined and dined the Centrum lander crew—not so intimately as Elvox, and not beyond discretion—and got into their good graces. Because she was obviously staying neutral, they had no objection to her tutoring Kawashita, and Kawashita had no objection to almost anything she did. By being pleasant and cooperative, she got her way.

The judgment of majority ownership was made in the Centrum lander, with all parties attending. The lander lounge was turned into a small courtroom, and the ten judges opened their records of deliberation. Elvox almost felt sorry for the Waunters. They looked totally defeated as they read the judgment. Alae's face was grim as death. She took her copy of the proceedings and walked out of the ship with Oomalo close behind.

Even after the judgment, the Centrum work wasn't over. It took two weeks for Centrum satellites to thoroughly scan the planet. Percentages of ownership had to be established, and values assigned for taxation.

In that time, Elvox's confusion seemed to evaporate. His time with Anna was smooth and regular. His awe at her status became subdued.

The planet yielded almost nothing—and what it did yield was an insult. The ruins of a weather machine were discovered practically at antipodes to the dome. Like the simulacra and equipment in the dome, the machine had powdered to a sandy mix of minerals and metal traces. How such a small device could control the weather was impossible to tell, but nothing else was found, and the ruin's outlines were at least suggestive of its purpose—field vanes, seeder guns, and the like. They analyzed the marks that resembled roadbeds, and found they were geological. The planet was still mildly active. The concrete plains were already being re-formed. In a hundred million years all traces of the Perfidisians would be buried or ground to rubble. It would be no great loss.

Of the nothing that the Perfidisians had left behind, Kawashita was given a ninety-percent interest. The Waunters, because of the unusual circumstances, were given a ten-percent share. The planet itself was to be controlled by Kawashita, but of any profits he might make from its eventual sale or lease or other dealings, ten percent would go to the Waunters. The Waunters could orbit and land anywhere on the planet they wished, at any time, so long as they did not interfere with operations that Kawashita could profit from. And so on, and on . . . all the fine legal points established over centuries of planetfalls and millennia of property settlements.

In the final proceedings, Kawashita didn't seem the least disappointed that he wasn't going to be wealthy.

"Has the majority owner decided on a name for this world?" the first judge asked him.

"I have," Kawashita said. "It will be known as Yamato."

Anna had coached him on the presentation, and he performed flawlessly.

"And does this name have a meaning?"

"Yes, your honors. It is the old name for my native land, Japan."

"Well and good. This court has made its decisions, executed its responsibilities as arbiter and mediator, and any further judgments must be appealed to Centrum courts on Myriadne. These proceedings are at an end."

Four hours later, the Waunters returned to their old Aighor ship and broke orbit.

TEN

"My God, Julio, you're an officer, not a Casanova!" Tivvers stood in the door to Elvox's cabin, hands on his hips, the perfect picture of outraged sensibility.

Elvox smiled wanly. "We're doing our work, aren't we? Nothing's slacked. All the decisions have been made."

"Yes—and you've found an excuse to keep us down here for another three weeks. Think the CO likes being delayed?"

Elvox stood in the cramped quarters and stretched. "We can help Kawashita readjust. We shouldn't just leave it to Anna and her crew."

"Why bother? This planet's stripped—worthless."

"I'm not so sure of that." He frowned and rubbed his head. "Call it a gut feeling."

"I call it being lovesick. She's got you right where she wants you. Let's up-ship and go to a righteous liberty, for Christ's sake—not this blasted billiard ball. You're the only one getting—"

"Goddammit, Tivvers, I'm your superior officer!"

Tivvers grinned sardonically. "Not that you'd notice by your actions."

"If you see me slacking, report it to the CO," Elvox said, bristling. He raised his hand and swept it to indicate the USC shuttle. "This is my command, and my decisions stand."

"She's using you."

"She is Anna Sigrid Nestor. She could have her pick of any man, and if she is settling for me, doesn't that mean something?"

"What?"

Elvox backed away and shrugged.

"She's got you bad, doesn't she? How the hell could you let this happen to yourself?"

"I'm a fool, I suppose," Elvox said blankly.

"What about that planet you come from, with all the zealots. Didn't any of their sense get through to you?"

Elvox rubbed his eyes and laughed. "Sense? Tivvers, they were Baptists and three or four other kinds of fool. They schismed from the lot that colonized God-Does-Battle, but they have the same goal—to bring Christian heaven down to Earth. Well, they couldn't have Earth, so they settled for Ichthys. Their idea of heaven doesn't include a rational approach to worldly things. God's kingdom is ruled by a line of patriarchs. That's what I grew up with, not sense. It was fine when I was a boy, but when the world started explaining itself to me through my gonads, it became hell. I thought I was a sex maniac, that my family would disown me. Well, I grew out of that but not completely. Not yet. I can't reject what I've been taught since I was a child."

"Then why is she getting to you?"

"Her attitude. She's so free and loving."

"Dross, pure dross. She's a businesswoman. She's using you for all you're worth."

For a moment Elvox seemed to be considering that. Then he shook his head. "No, she's helping me to grow up. She's not the first woman I've had, not by a long shot. But—"

"She's got you, all right."

"I will not give her up easily! I feel like I'm willing to give everything to her."

"Concessions."

Elvox shook his head. "You're a block of ice, Tivvers."

"No, I'm an officer, and I'm your friend. This is going to cook your career if it goes any further."

Elvox pushed past the unterloytnant and took the ladder down to the equipment bay. Tivvers followed, keeping quiet, trying to figure out what he was up to.

"I'm going to her ship," he said.

"You've been staying here off and on to keep up appearances, right?" Tivvers said. Elvox didn't answer.

On the concrete, walking to Nestor's shuttle, he felt a sudden dislike for Kawashita. He envied the Japanese and his immediate access to Nestor. They were all so concerned with Kawashita, but he was little more than a freak.

Elvox shook his head vigorously. They'd have to leave soon. He'd have to make his decision. Nestor would take the Japanese to Earth for a visit, fulfilling her obligations as a guide and tutor. And Elvox? He couldn't stand the thought of returning to normal duty. But lately the idea of joining Anna's crew had seemed—as Tivvers would undoubtedly comment if he knew—a bit off the beam.

The last few days she had seemed more reluctant, preoccupied. Was that because of Kawashita? His thoughts were jumbled. Separation. Disgrace. Disgust. What the hell was he doing?

His bubble merged with the environment around the ramp. The russet-furred alter stood at the top of the ramp, arms folded. Elvox looked away from her animal femininity. She was one of the few that had stayed behind after another shuttle had picked up Nestor's entourage. "Can I help you, Loytnant?" she asked, her beautiful voice incongruously human.

"I'd like to speak to Anna."

The alter called Nestor to the intercom.

"Julio!" Anna's voice, over the speaker, sounded tired. "Listen, things are really hell around here. We're making all the final preparations. We leave in four days. Will you—be coming with us?"

"I don't know," he said, suddenly feeling unclean. "I'll have to see you soon." He couldn't have told Tivvers about the offer. It would have meant cutting the last thin threads of respect still between them.

"I've got a lot of questions," he said, looking down at the concrete.

The alter seemed to regard him with pity.

"Fine. Come tomorrow morning. I'll have some clear time then."

That night he was almost sick.

The next morning he was mad but still queasy. He said nothing to Tivvers as he left the lander, and Tivvers kept his counsel to himself.

It was time to have things out.

ELEVEN

"I have run out of things to see about the new Earth," Kawashita said.

"There's much more on the main ship," Nestor said.

"I do not know if I'm prepared for Japan."

"I haven't seen Earth myself for fifteen years."

Kawashita smiled. "A blink," he said.

"Sometimes I think you enjoy being a Methuselah."

"A Rip van Winkle, you mean."

"Enjoy the hell out of it."

Kawashita's smile faded. "No. Not always."

"I don't see how you could have done anything harmful when you were alone for four hundred years."

"Not to others who were real, perhaps—but they saw themselves as real. I felt a great deal for some of them, and what I did hurt them much. Some I had killed."

"You were half-crazy."

"No," Kawashita said. "I was sane. I did everything with excuses. I had history to follow and did not have the strength to break loose. I wanted to create a better place, but—" He shrugged. "Perhaps later I can tell it straightly."

Anna looked out the direct view port at the USC lander. "I think it must be impossible not to hurt people."

"What will you do about him?"

She gave him a sharp look. "You see an awful lot," she said, "even when you seem to look the other way."

"Remember, I was a high-ranking official for many decades."

"Don't presume too much, Yoshio. You're more responsible than a trained monkey. You're still a human." Her glare softened suddenly and she shuddered. "Oh, God, I'm sorry. That was unforgivably blunt. There's a lot of poison in me, too."

"He is very involved in you."

"When I first saw him, I thought I could feel strongly, too. But it hasn't turned out that way. Physically, in most other ways, he's everything I want in a man . . . but there's something weak in him. Not just weak, more . . ." She gestured the thought away.

"It is unwise to play with a man when you are not certain how you feel."

Anna sparked again. "Dammit, this is none of your business!"

"True," Yoshio said, his face impassive.

"I offered him a position on the ship. Now I don't think he's good for the job. Sometimes I'm a complete ass, and I don't know why."

"Maybe you are crazy," Kawashita said.

"No," Anna said, turning away. "I had my reasons. I did everything . . . with excuses. My shame."

"It is not unusual for people to be hurt by loves that do not work," Kawashita said. "It is a part of growth, not like betrayal."

"Sometimes it seems very much a betrayal, though," she mused. "Like giving promises without meaning them."

"When the body rules, souls die. Loss of love is like grieving for the death of a person who never was."

"I don't love him," Nestor said. "He may not even love me. Maybe my vanity is imagining it all."

Kawashita shook his head. "Kill it quickly," he said. "Don't settle for anything but a mortal wound, a quick end."

Anna avoided his eyes. But she understood what he meant.

TWELVE

When she let him in, she wouldn't look at him, and his insides seemed to turn to ice. He straightened himself and went to the cabin they had shared so often. She walked just behind him, robes swishing back and forth. She had lost some of her vitality. Elvox didn't say anything until they were alone and the door was shut.

"What happened yesterday?" he asked, trying to be cheerful and casual. She smiled weakly and said everything had been worked out. Then she told him that Kawashita wanted to see Japan.

"Won't be anything like what he remembers," he said.

"Some parts are still preserved," she said. "But he knows how different it will be."

"What does he want to wander for? Why not just settle here and tend his property?"

She laughed a short, hard laugh. "There's nothing here. Even his memories are falling apart with the stuff in the dome."

"It's just about gone now." Elvox said.

"I hope we'll part as friends."

"I've never known anyone like you," he said, almost in the same instant. "I've been wanting to—"

"Clarify," she said. "All this should be made clear."

"Yes."

"A lark," she said.

"Not to me." He felt his eyes water and resisted the pressure. "Very serious."

"We gave each other relaxation in a hard time."

"That's all?"

"And affection. I appreciate it."

"What was so hard about it? You got everything you wanted."

"Which turned out to be nothing."

"You got me."

"Julio, it isn't—"

"It was," he said. They were quiet for a few moments. "Given time."

"Not for me." And that was it. He had to salvage something, so he said, "Not expedient, hm? I couldn't accept a position on your ship, anyway. I have better opportunities elsewhere."

"Of course."

"I can see where you might have a lot of work to do. I'd only be in the way." She did feel for him, Elvox thought, more than she was letting on—but something had come up. That was it. A stronger motive was making her back away. "Kawashita knows more, right?"

"What are you talking about?"

"I'll leave. I won't even report it."

"Report what?"

"The Waunters will never hear of it."

"Jesus Christ, what are you talking about?"

He left the cabin, bumping past Kawashita on the way to the cargo lock. He gave the Japanese a wild, desperate glance, almost a question, then made his features blank and walked quickly down the ramp. He picked up his environment pack and pushed through the bubble. Nestor watched from the cargo lock, tears welling in her eyes, feeling like the youngest, cruelest child. She shrugged off Kawashita's hand and ran to the left to go to the bridge.

Elvox gave terse orders and sent a quick message to the orbiting USC ship. "Our job's done here," he told Tivvers. "They're leaving in a few days. Kawashita's going with them. Everything's okay, no problems, so why should we stay." His voice was level. Tivvers nodded.

"There's a lot of work to do before we go," Elvox said.

THIRTEEN

Kawashita sat on the edge of the sleep-field, in the dark, thinking about what he had said to Nestor and what she had said back. She was a strong-willed woman but not cruel. Still, she could cause pain.

He held his hands over his eyes, though it didn't make the surroundings any darker. He tried to count his fingers.

His daughter, in the world beneath the dome, had been a strong-willed woman, whose recognition of necessity drove her to court machinations, and finally to murder. Masa had held all the evil inherent in living packed tight in her small body. She had stopped him when he tried to step out of history. Their final contest had resulted in a slaughter so disgusting the *kami* had abandoned him.

For three years he had lived alone—with Ko, he knew, he had been alone—surrounded by the evidence of his folly. He could not force the scene to change. Everything necessary to keep him alive still operated, but nothing more.

Perhaps his plans had failed because of his eternal youth. He could not behave like an old man, no matter how much experience and wisdom accumulated in him, for his body always reacted like the body of a young man. In his years of loneliness he'd learned how to control some of those reactions, saving his sanity; but now the constraints were off. How should he behave in a culture where sexual proscriptions appeared to be few and far between? The encounters between the woman and the United Stars officer had bothered him because he didn't have the courage—or the knowledge—to find his own companion. He still wasn't familiar with protocol and social behavior to take such a risk.

He ordered the lights to turn on again and went into the lavatory to look over the equipment. Somehow the variety soothed him. It was so alien, so fascinating. But one piece still bothered him.

"How is that used?" he asked, pointing to the cylinder with the phallus and vagina. He had long since learned the voices weren't human, so he wasn't embarrassed to ask questions.

"It's a device for solitary release, fantasy encounters, or noncontact encounters."

"How?"

"A request is placed, and if the request matches that of someone else on the circuit, you may engage in a noncontact encounter. Holograms of each participant are projected around the tube, and the full sensations of sexual contact are mimicked. If you wish a fantasy encounter, you may select from a multitude of stored sequences. Solitary release can be achieved in several ways."

He wrinkled his nose and left the lavatory. He wasn't ready to couple with ghosts again. He ordered the lights out and activated the sleep-field. Despite a lulling vibration effect, he had a difficult two hours of restlessness before he slept.

In the morning Nestor chimed on his door to wake him in time to see the USC ship launch. "It's going up in twenty minutes," she said. "Since you've never seen a spacecraft launch before, I thought you'd be interested."

"Yes, very much."

"Let's go outside. There's no danger at this distance, and you'll get the full effect that way."

The brass-colored, bullet-shaped lander rested on its extension pads, flat belly toward them, bottom ports showing the motion of several men in the control center. The Perfidisian planet was giving a bright send-off, with skies almost blue and sun almost bright enough to warm the air. All they required were skin suits and breathers, and as environmental fields would have "dulled the effect," Nestor subjected him to the slight discomfort of suit up.

The ports were opaqued, and a sharp klaxon warned of imminent takeoff. The ground vibrated underfoot, but he couldn't see a thing. He knew the landers weren't powered by chemical-fuel rockets—he'd read the manual and understood at least that much. But something, he reasoned, had to boost them up and out. He thought it would come from the bottom, so he kept his eyes trained there. The ship began to glow all around. The concrete beneath it hissed and popped as it expanded. With a sustained whine that grew louder and deeper at once, the lander rose slowly for ten or twelve meters, then more rapidly. It vanished with a scream, leaving a plugged sensation in his ears.

"What do they feel inside?" he asked when the noise had died.

"You'll see," Nestor said. "Nothing drastic, so don't worry. But you're going to experience a lot of new feelings before this week is out."

Kawashita nodded. "That is something I think about but am not sure what to think."

"Frightened?" Nestor asked.

He shook his head. "What is there to be frightened of?" he asked. "It's been a long time since anything frightened me."

FOURTEEN

"It's as big as the Perfidisian ship," Kawashita said, looking at the image of Nestor's vessel on the lounge screens. "And it has teardrop shapes on struts . . . just the same." His voice was shaky.

"No coincidence. It's a practical design for ships built to travel through higher spaces. Don't ask me why, though. I leave that to my engineers."

"I've never seen the stars so clear before."

"Give us magnification two thousand on the nine-W-nine-N square," Anna requested. The screen fogged, then cleared, and a bright wreath of gas appeared, surrounded by the stars of the galactic disk. "That's the Lily, a supernova remnant. Beautiful, no? And valuable. She has a few planets still, one of them the stripped core of a gas-giant. United Stars has a mining operation on that world—Kiril, what's the name of the Lily's mining planet?"

"Amargosa," the pilot answered through the intercom.

"Amargosa strained the supernova cloud of quite a sampling of superheavy elements, all useful in warper-ship technology. But her surface is made of solid hydrogen. The central city has to be isolated by thermal shields. I've never been there—USC has never invited me—but someday I'd like to see it. Back to full screen. Now look just beyond the shadow of the ship—see that ring of stars? They're surrounded by fields of radiation so intense they can't be approached through normal space. And if a ship tries to get to them through higher spaces, she's never heard from again. We suspect it's an Aighor stronghold, but we don't know whether Aighors are still there. The Centrum is negotiating with them right now to find out what's going on. It could be dangerous to have a phenomenon like that in our midst and be completely wrong about what it is."

"There is so much to see," Kawashita said wistfully. "In the beginning I thought perhaps I was dead. The dense region of stars—from Earth, it is still called the Milky Way?"

Nestor nodded.

"In my Japan there were stories about the Milky Way. It was called Heaven's River. On one side was a woman weaving, on the other a lover who could cross the river only on the seventh night of the seventh moon. And some thought that when you died, you crossed the river to become a star. I crossed Heaven's River, yet I didn't die. Can I expect much more out of life after a miracle like that?"

"Don't see why not," Anna said. "You didn't get to do much sight-seeing along the way."

Kawashita shook his head and grinned. "I wonder whether you have much poetry in your soul."

Anna mirrored his smile, a particularly ambiguous response. "Women don't need to be poets, not as much as men."

"In Japan some of the best poets were women. The men were too busy with wars and politics."

"Well, maybe I'm a man at heart. My poetry lies in what I do. My ambition is to give other people reasons to be poetic, and time to do it in. In return, I have a certain amount of freedom to do and be what I please. I'm not dry inside, though. I'm just not very good at putting my thoughts into words."

The pilot interrupted. "Docking in three minutes. We've already had six requests for matched quarters with Yoshio."

"Well?" Anna asked the Japanese.

"Matched quarters?"

"Is there anyone you'd like to share a room with?"

Kawashita thought it over for a moment, then shook his head back and forth once, quickly. "Not yet."

Anna nodded. "He's not taking offers yet." She turned back to Kawashita. "You know, that means they'll accuse me of keeping you to myself."

"But we have not—"

"Gossip doesn't feed on truth. Don't worry, though. It can't tarnish my reputation any more."

"I apologize for inconvenience."

"Docked," the pilot announced.

"Not at all," Anna said. "Welcome to my home away from home."

Only a small portion of Anna's entourage had come to the planet's surface with her. The rest had stayed in their various quarters, laboratories, and studios, going about life as though nothing unusual were happening. A few came to the lander bay to meet the boarding party, and among them was one of the furred tecto alters Kawashita had seen before. She kept her gaze on him and he was confused. Nestor took him by the arm, introduced him around, and led him out of the bay. "We call it *Peloros*. One of my more extravagant tools and toys."

"Peloros was a monster," Kawashita said, looking at the robot conveyors on the other side of the corridor's glass partition.

"True, but another Peloros was a navigator of great skill. I like the mix. My father suggested it before the ship was built. You are now an official guest, and protocol demands I give you the best. But the best is a bit too rich even for my blood, and you probably won't be used to it, so you have a choice."

"I was just getting used to your cabin in the lander."

"That's Spartan fare, Yoshio. Only my ascetic friends live in such deprived surroundings. But maybe something can be arranged."

"I begin to feel homesick," Kawashita said. "Actually, I've been homesick for some time now. It is probably crazy, but I had peace in the dome, after the Perfidisians went away. Much time to think. Now I have a flood of thinking to do, and too little time to do it in. Can I have just a place to rest, recuperate? And a tapas pad. And food I am used to."

Nestor nodded at each request. "Easily arranged. I was kidding—not all of us are sybaritic. A lot of useful work gets done on board. I don't put up with people who waste time."

"What will I do as guest? How will I pay my way?"

They came to the corridor's end, a wider hall lined on each side and on the ceiling with hatches leading to cabins. Nestor didn't answer for a moment, and there was an awkward silence.

"You can keep us entertained, I suppose, telling about

old history. Stories of life in the dome. But most of all, for my pleasure, you can survive and try to be content. One part of me says that a man who has roots as far in the past as you do won't be able to stand our cultures. He'll go crazy. There are ways of repairing him, but he won't be the same. But you aren't going crazy. You're adapting, and rather well. That fascinates me. You improve my view of humanity, and that's a valuable gift. You're also a planetholder, which makes you a potential business partner. No matter how barren a planet might be on first look, someone, somewhere, will think of a use. You control how your planet will be used, and if you control it wisely, we all benefit."

"Which comes first," Kawashita asked, "human interest or mercenary?"

"Personally, human interest. As a free-lance adviser, the mercenary aspects can't be ignored. Socially, there's prestige in having you as my guest. Take your pick of any aspect—there are a lot more. I haven't bothered to sort them out." She cocked her head to one side and lifted the corners of her lips with the barest indication of a smile. "Our cultures may be more complex, but the people probably aren't. A lot of what you knew on Earth and in the dome still applies. I'm interested to see how you apply it." She took a small card from her pocket and handed it to him. "Your room is number forty-five on the right side of the hall. Going in and out, pay attention to the access light above the hatch. You can tell whether someone is leaving the room above you, and avoid bumping into him, her, or . . . it. No it's this voyage."

He held up the card. "This is a key."

"Hold it in whichever hand you're most inclined to use, leave it there for thirty seconds, then slip it into the notch under the access light. That keys you into the room. Only you can open the hatch by touching the entrance panel— except in an emergency, of course. If you wish, you can key it to voice activation. The machines will explain themselves. Forty-five is an adjustable cabin. It'll do anything you tell it to, short of expanding. Make it as spare as you wish. When you've gotten used to it, I'd like you to join me on the bridge for dinner."

"When do we leave?"

"We already have. A few hours after dinner, we'll enter higher spaces."

Kawashita nodded and watched her walk down the long corridor back to the vehicle bay. Then he entered his room. When he opened the door, he saw that the closet was putting away his clothes for him.

FIFTEEN

The old Aighor ship was silent and cold. Water dripped softly in the sea-tanks that circumnavigated the midriff, and a small motor in the engine sentry systems whined briefly, but the usual sounds of ship life were absent. The old weapons storage chambers were littered with equipment, and scaffoldings had been set up along the sixty-meter inboard bulkhead, but there was no one to put them to use.

Two kilometers outside the ship, the Waunters inspected their last two weeks' work. The lander swung in a slow, lazy arc around the green hulk. Its occupants watched the screens in a kind of stupor.

"We should go back inside. It's all done," Oomalo said.

"Why even bother to do maintenance?" Alae asked. "What will we do when we get back? Nobody's commissioned us. We're not listeners unless we have a commission."

"We don't need one. Nothing's wrong with the ship. Systems will last another two hundred years before they incur any expense."

"Two hundred years," Alae said. "I don't think I want to live that long."

"Wait until we get back to routine. We can do basic research. We're free-lance, remember. We can peddle information without a commission."

Alae nodded absently. "I'd like to shift the quarters around. Open up new rooms and move into them. Have fresh surroundings. The old rooms make my guts ache."

Oomalo agreed to that. "If nothing else," he said, "you can help me explore and record the ship. There's an awful lot left to do."

"Nothing useful," she said. "Nothing we can sell."

"Probably not. The Crocerians wouldn't have sold it to

us if they thought anything unusual was in it. But who knows?"

"Every ten years, for the next two hundred years, we'll go out and inspect the ship all around, plant new monitors on the hull, live our lives, and nothing will happen. Does that sound like much of a life to you?"

"We could always go back, sell the ship now. I'm sure we could get a good price for it. It's a good ship."

"Big. Like a world. I've lived in it too long to be happy where other people are. The quiet gets in my blood, settles the waves. I'll be okay. Let's go back and start shifting things around."

"That's better," Oomalo said. "Back to routine. We'll start listening on our own tomorrow."

"Back to routine," Alae said slowly. "Peace."

SIXTEEN

"I have two thousand people on the *Peloros,*" Nestor said, laying out the hard-copy plans on a table for Kawashita to see. "Five hundred crew and researchers—only about ten active crew, but the roles mix sometimes—and fifteen hundred friends, hangers-on, artists, entertainers. Mostly I keep them around to gauge their reactions when we find something new."

"How often is that?"

"Two or three times a voyage. We've scouted a thousand systems in this ship and explored about a hundred. We've found fifteen habitable worlds, five without indigenous life forms. The other ten we turned over to the care of the Galactic Social Engineers. They make sure nobody bothers the natives until they're ready to join the fun on their own. We put survey teams on the other five, mapped and charted and sampled them, and staked claims. Some of the information we sold to a few consolidations, some to the Centrum. We even sold information to Hafkan Bestmerit for a genealogical survey."

"How was that?"

"A million years ago the Aighors developed interstellar travel—that is, an ancestral species did. In a short time they got into a war with the Minkies and destroyed about fifty civilized worlds. God knows why they went to war. Peaceful coexistence is so much cheaper, and there's room enough for everybody but the most die-hard propagationist. Even then, and the Galaxy was more crowded at the time. At any rate, they reduced each other to prespace technology. That was the first-stage Aighor civilization.

"The second stage rediscovered interstellar travel and made an experiment. They took several dozen intelligent species, still locked on their home worlds, and transplanted them by force to other planets. Nobody appreciated that, and when the Aighor watchdogs over the experimental planets became lax, some of the transplants developed space technologies and attacked them.

"That was the end of the second stage. Because of that, the lineage of a lot of species has been called into question. We found three far-flung vestiges, relatives of groups still active in Hafkan Bestmerit. One had survived with only prespace technology. The other two had sunk even lower, down to minimal existences, completely overcome by the natural planetary ecologies. Some species are still pressing a kind of lawsuit against the Aighors, and in the interest of unity within Hafkan Bestmerit, the Aighors are complying with the judgments."

"Hafkan Bestmerit is the only consolidation with no human members?"

"If it can strictly be called a consolidation. It's a rather exclusive group. Aighors, Minkies, Crocerians, and—some think—Perfidisians. But there's no evidence Perfidisians associate with anyone. We guess there are about twenty distinct species within Hafkan Bestmerit, some of whom we know little about."

"These Aighors, are they totally irrational?" Kawashita said.

"Not at all. They're among the most inventive and intelligent species we've met. They're aggressive, but then they developed from a background where extreme aggression was the only way to survive. Still, we're lucky they didn't find us before we were ready to compete."

"But they destroyed their civilization several times."

"That's not unheard of," Anna said. "We've found the remains of four thousand spacefaring civilizations, of which maybe a hundred are going concerns today. That appears to be the norm, judging from transmissions received from other galaxies."

"You have not traveled between galaxies?"

"Only to the Magellans. A few exploratory ships are planned. But higher space warps depend to a certain extent on large local bodies of mass for guidance. The distances between the galaxies are forbidding because they're practically empty. On the other hand, we've yet to investigate the galactic core because the stars are too densely packed. I've heard the Aighors have a way of navigating hyperdense and hypodense geodesics—"

"Excuse me," Kawashita said. "I can't keep pace looking up definitions on the tapas."

"Don't worry. You're doing fine. I understand a lot less than I know, myself. Poetic imagery is the only way some of these ideas can be grasped, unless you're hooked up to a computer with specially augmented circuitry."

"Back to the Aighors. Have you had a war with them yet?"

"Some skirmishes but no official wars. We may not be especially adept, but we do develop fast, and our technology is the equal of theirs, point for point—at least in transportable weapons and shields. They may have something—but no, that's top secret. I'm not supposed to know about it."

Kawashita grinned. "Now I am curious."

Anna suddenly resembled a little girl about to divulge a secret. "Don't tell anyone," she said. "But we found parts of some of the ships that went into the Ring Stars. Not my group—humans, though. Something very odd had happened to the scraps. I'm not sure what it was, but one older physicist had a heart attack when he saw them."

Kawashita shook his head slowly; whether in disbelief or wonder, Anna couldn't tell. "Do you believe in gods?" he asked.

"I don't disbelieve in anything. I've seen too much to be a complete agnostic, so I suppose I do believe in something, yes."

"When I was a young boy, my mother let me attend a Christian Sunday school service in Hiroshima. It was taught by an old Jesuit from Spain, and he said that someday, when men looked far enough into space with their telescopes, they would see the face of God glowering at them. Have you seen anything like that?"

Anna smiled. "I'm sorry to be rude, but you're still asking quaint questions. Not bad ones—just quaint. We have legends. Lost ships, planets that disappear when they're landed, paradises—but they're fairy tales for the most part."

"For a Japanese from my time, the universe would be filled with *kami*," he said. "Aighors would be *kami,* and so would Perfidisians. *Kami* are not the same as the Christian God, but they are intelligent beings, special ancestors, spirits sometimes, not omnipotent, however. And every star is a goddess, every world a pearl. Does that give you awe?"

Anna paused. "Sometimes I think I'm too dense to be awed," she said, "or too busy having fun. But somewhere, yes, I suppose I'm a little scared of it all."

"I've been lucky, coming to see it gradually," Kawashita said. "The person who was a pilot, back in the twentieth century—he would be mad by now. Me, I am just made nervous most of the time."

"Welcome to the world-anxiety of the modern human," Anna said, laughing. "Some night, come to my observation bubble and look at the magnified and annotated stars with me. Be prepared to shiver a little. We haven't scratched the surface yet. Maybe God's face will glower down on us some day. Maybe at the Galaxy's core."

"No, there are six wings at the Galaxy's core," Kawashita said cryptically. Anna couldn't get him to explain what he meant, but it seemed a kind of joke.

She pointed out the ship's engines on the chart and asked if he'd like to do something he could only do once.

"It does not sound pleasant," he said. " 'Once a philosopher, twice a pervert,' as Voltaire said."

"Oh, it isn't dangerous, and it doesn't change you any way you'd notice. But you can only do it once."

"I'll decide when I see what it is."

She took him down the long tube separating the living quarters from the vehicle bays and engines, then pointed him through a round hatch into a room gleaming with bare metal surfaces. The rest of the *Peloros* was decorated with a variety of coordinated color schemes, but here, at its heart, there was no speck of color. A steel-gray cube approached and asked their business. Anna held her hand out for identification and requested its presence at an initiation. Apparently she had done this sort of thing before; the cube complied without objection. It led them down another tube to a weightless spherical chamber. A transparent globe was suspended in the center. Kawashita felt a gluey kind of force fingering him as they floated toward the sphere, like moving through webs of invisible gelatin. His hair stood on end, and his eyes flashed with sparks when he closed them.

Anna, resembling a comedy harridan, took his hand and

pressed it against the transparent surface of the sphere. "It's not glass," she said. "It isn't even matter. It's a field of probabilities. It dictates that the chances your hand will pass through it are zero. So you can't pass through. But there's a way." She told the cube to open a test hole.

"At the center of the probability zone is something which makes up about one third of the ship's mass. You were reading about black holes a few wake-periods ago, weren't you?"

Kawashita nodded. "Something was said about their use in ship's engines."

"Then you read about black holes separating virtual particles out of space and radiating energy."

"Virtual particles—they are the ones that are always being created and destroyed, but so fast nothing can detect them?"

"Right—created in pairs of opposites, and they annihilate each other after being created, so the total energy content of the universe is stable. Around a black hole, however, a pair of virtual particles can be separated before they annihilate each other. One particle falls below the event horizon—which nothing can escape from—and the other escapes as created energy. But that defies the conservation of energy, so we have to think of the particle that fell into the black hole as actually emerging in reversed time. It's much more complicated than that, but what it means is a black hole radiates energy. The smaller the hole, the *brighter* it is—until we get down to quantum black holes. At the center of the sphere there's a collapsed mass about the size of an electron. But size doesn't mean much down there because we protect ourselves by wrapping it in thirty or forty layers of probability—"

"Thirty-seven this voyage, madam," the cube said.

"Right. Each layer is equal to a self-contained universe, each with its own separate rules and constants. Every opposite layer has precisely the reverse character of the layers above and beneath it. Nothing can interact between regions with qualities and constants so drastically different. The final layer, surrounding the hole, puts enormous pressure on it—in effect, makes it probable the black hole will radiate several trillion times more energy than it naturally should. This makes it leak out through itself—a concept I've never understood—and from that leakage below the Planck-Wheeler length—"

"Pardon," Kawashita said, bringing up his tapas.

"Something like ten to the minus thirty-three centimeters," Anna said. "Much smaller than an electron. Anyway, we get our power from the leakage. The interesting thing—and it can only be done once—is to reach in and touch the outermost probability field."

Kawashita looked doubtful. "Why can it only be done once?"

"Touch it once, nothing happens to you. But touch it twice—with a lapse of several minutes—and it increases your chances of dying. Don't ask me how—it has to do with Parakem functions and world-line energy theorems. I've done it. It's an initiation for spacefarers, like crossing the equator used to be for seafarers on Earth."

"What does it feel like?"

"Not painful. You asked about seeing the face of God. Well, this isn't quite as spectacular, but it'll do until Judgment Day."

Kawashita nodded reluctantly. He didn't want to seem afraid, and he understood the idea so little that he didn't know whether to be afraid or not. Anna guided him to the rift in the sphere using the hand wires strung across the chamber. She guided his hand through the gap. "Reach in to the black spot in the middle—looks like a marble."

He slowly brought his finger close to the center.

"You have ten seconds to touch it—touch it however many times you want, without taking your finger more than a few centimeters from the center. It really amounts to touching it once. Go ahead."

His finger made contact. "It's moving," he said. "Everything's moving." He looked around the chamber nervously. Anna was haloed with rainbows and lightnings. Her eyes were pits of ice and fire. The cube was surrounded by flashing feathers of light. Angels, thrones, dominations, and cherubim. *Kami.* The walls were covered with neon signs of such complexity he couldn't begin to analyze them; they were layered with *katakana* figures, numbers, and insignia. He could see through his arm, and at the center of his bones he saw a thin line of black, which opened onto elongated stars, a cosmos within his marrow. Then something pushed his finger away, and he floated in the round chamber, shaking, smiling, and finally crying. *"Me ga areba, miru koto go dekimasen!"* he said through his sobbing. "We can see if we have eyes!"

Anna grasped his arm and pushed him out of the chamber. She was frightened by his reaction. He seemed to be coming apart, breaking into a babbling child. "I've been an *idiot,*" she hissed. "Oh, Jesus, Buddha, and Lords!"

She punched an emergency button on the way to Kawashita's quarters. "Get a physics cube and a human doctor down here, forty-five port quarters, immediately!"

She guided him into his room and lay him down on the sleep-field. He shut his eyes. *"Me o tojireba nani mo miemasen."*

"What did he say?" she asked his tapas.

" 'If we close our eyes, we cannot see anything,' " the tapas translated.

The cube floated in, and Dr. Henderson followed immediately after. The cube dropped down and hovered over Kawashita's hand. Anna held her knuckles to her teeth. "I was stupid, stupid, *stupid.* I didn't even think of what the Perfidisians could have done to him. Maybe this was his second time!"

SEVENTEEN

"I don't care how safe it is, I've never liked the idea. There are a hell of a lot of things we don't know." Henderson stood by the edge of the sleep-field, rubbing his forehead with a thick-fingered hand. "I'm not sure what happened to him, but the attendant cube would have detected him if he'd done anything similar before."

"You touched it six years ago," Nestor said.

"Under social duress, yes."

"You know what happens. Why did he behave differently?"

He shook his head and ordered the physics cube to leave the cabin. "Anna, you're not dealing with an inhabitant of the twenty-fourth century. He's probably never even looked at his phosphene patterns, much less the backside of his skull. We're used to complex intoxication—to us, it's a safe and reasonable science. But in his day, if it occurred at all, it was regarded as a religious experience."

"I understand that. I joked about him seeing the face of God."

"Whatever he saw, it pushed him over into a temporary seizure. Not that he's epileptic; he just locked his doors and decided to retreat for a few minutes. Do you understand what happens when we touch the hole?"

Anna shook her head. "Not completely."

"I won't chide you for your ignorance. But if you're going to play with something so powerful, at least try to know what's going on. That's common sense, right?"

Anna nodded.

"When we touch it, we come in contact with a weak outer field of probability, which dictates that our nervous system will behave with greater efficiency than normal. The result is a kind of superstimulus—we become sensitive to everything. Blake called it opening the doors of perception. It's not unlike what happens when we pass through warp."

"I think he was asleep when we entered warp the first time."

"He didn't talk about it?"

"No. He was on the inducer that evening. He was too keyed up to sleep naturally."

"Next time, let him get used to our fun and games through easy introductions. Can you explain all this to him?"

"I think so," Anna said meekly.

"Can you explain why he should never touch the hole again?"

"No."

"It's simple. Next time the field will behave exactly in reverse. His nervous system will suffer reduced efficiency. All his vital functions will stop. He'll be dead before a medical cube can reach him." Henderson looked down at Kawashita. "I've always wondered what somebody who's never lived in our society would think of us. They'd probably decide we're still children. We still do silly, dangerous things for ridiculous reasons. Right?" He looked sternly at Nestor.

She shivered. "Right," she said.

"Like children. We never really grow up."

"That's enough, Henderson," she said. "I've got your point. No need to grind it in."

"As you wish. Is the hole off limits, even for initiations?"

She nodded.

"He'll come out of it soon. I can stay with him, if you have other things to do, but he needs to have someone around him for a while."

"I'll stay."

The doctor left Kawashita's cabin. Nestor pulled her robes out around her knees and sat on the chair, looking at Kawashita's face, still touched by a slight inclination of the eyebrows, a squinting of the eyes, but quiet now and almost peaceful.

"It creeps up on us, and we don't even suspect," she whispered to his sleeping form. "It takes someone like you to trip us up and show our flaws. We owe a great deal to the innocents."

She sat by the bed for an hour, watching the rhythmic motion of his chest, the taps of pulse in his wrist and in a vein near his temple. "You're not a tame monkey any more," she said. "You're not my toy." Then she felt a rise of heat in her throat, and she hated herself more intensely than she had in years.

Yoshio stirred on the sleep-field and murmured something in Japanese. His eyes opened and he stiffened, then relaxed.

"You were dreaming," Anna said, smiling down on him.

"I went to visit a friend," he said.

"Who was that?"

"A man who tutored my daughter."

"Tutored Masa?"

"Yes, a wise gentleman who tried to warn me about her, that she was not going to behave the way I wished her to behave. Before she married Yoritomo."

"What happened?"

"It was only a dream," Kawashita said.

"Dreams are important."

"He said I was free now, I did not have to search."

"For what?"

"A reason why I did the things I did."

"Why shouldn't you search anymore?"

"Because there is no one to demand satisfactory answers. When I put my finger on the black hole, I saw things clear, and all the complexity behind them. But there was no spirit waiting to ask questions."

"You didn't see the face of God. Don't be disappointed—it really isn't that sort of thing."

"You do not understand. I saw the face, but it wasn't asking questions. It was waiting."

"For what?"

"I don't know." He turned his head away and closed his eyes. "When I was a child, I saw a demon. It scared me so badly I never went into that room again, not willingly. It was the room where my grandmother slept. But she had died recently, and without my knowing it, my parents changed all the furniture. I woke up from a nap, dreaming about grandmother, and went to her room to tell her about it. I forgot she wasn't with us anymore. When I opened the door and walked in, everything was different, and I couldn't understand why. I looked at the different furniture, the new prints on the wall, and became frightened. I had never seen the room before. It was like I had opened a door into another world, a nightmare place. I accepted that so completely that I looked into a corner and saw a demon squatting there, staring at me. He looked like a frog with horns and had a man's legs, and his eyes were huge and white, like a blind fish's. He stood up—he was half as tall as I—and came at me with sharp claws. I screamed and ran away. When I stopped running, I was in the kitchen, alone, with nothing chasing me. Now I know where the frog-demon is." He tapped his chest. "Me. I am the one who has crossed over into the wrong world, not a little boy. Divine spirits abducted me, tested me, and found me wanting. So now there is no reason to look for answers."

"I don't follow you," Anna said.

"Since no one wants to know why I did such things, I only have to satisfy myself. That makes me happier."

"Are you feeling all right?"

Kawashita smiled. "A little confused, weak. But much better, yes."

"You scared me. You still scare me. All this talk about demons and divine spirits. I thought we were joking about seeing God's face."

"Yes," Kawashita said flatly. "It was a joke."

"I'll never understand the punch line, then."

"When East meets West—even so extended a West as you are—it's like different species meeting, no?" Kawashita held out his hand and patted her cheek gently. "We are what you call unknowable?"

"Inscrutable," Nestor supplied.

"But don't worry. Show me Earth, let me learn, let me find my own way."

"I won't stop you," she said. "I'm too curious."

EIGHTEEN

The warm brown line of sunrise was so beautiful it made him ache inside. He could follow dawn's progress, imagine the daylight hitting cities and towns, graying skies, closing night flowers and opening day flowers, closing owl's eyes and opening people's eyes. Beneath the clouds, woven over the green lands and blue-black seas, were many white specks he knew weren't snow-capped mountains. He asked Anna what they were.

"Cities," she said.

"But I see them on the horizon, like bumps."

"Some are pretty big," she said. "Bigger than mountains, anyway."

"They're everywhere."

"You've gone through the tapas, haven't you?"

"Yes, but they aren't the same. This is real."

Anna floated to the center of the bridge bubble and shielded her eyes against Earth's glare. "Look off to thirty degrees, just beyond the edge of the ship's hull."

He pressed against the transparent material and followed the line of her finger. There was a tiny sparkle of light floating in space, which he could just barely resolve into a circle if he squinted. "What is it?"

"The first space station to carry a permanent staff. One hundred fifty meters across—tiny little thing. It's kept as a museum now. It was hoisted—let's see—fifty years after you left Earth. You might have lived to see it."

"I *have* lived to see it," Kawashita said. "There are advantages to being a Rip van Winkle."

"If we sit here much longer, we'll probably see five or ten ships in parking orbits. It's a crowded sky."

Three landers were prepared, each carrying fifty passengers. The *Peloros* carried only a few tons of material cargo, which was being prepared for ship-to-surface transmission. Nestor took Kawashita into the transmission chamber and pointed out the items that could legally be broken down into energy and radiated to surface receivers for reconstruction.

"I have six works of art from a human colony around Epsilon Eridani. Certified original works have tagged atoms implanted in them which scramble a signal so they can't be transmitted. Exotic materials—organics, perfumes, drugs, and so on—are difficult to transmit because their structures haven't been completely analyzed, and loss of detail can be disastrous. Humans and anything but the simplest living things are forbidden by law—not because we can't send them down and re-create them but for philosophical reasons.

"I've been told that anyone who understands how matter is put together doesn't have any doubts that received and original objects are the same, but there's a big emotional question involved. Most members of Hafkan Bestmerit allow transmission of known living creatures, but by Earth standards that's barbaric. Myself, I'm not so certain—but I won't volunteer for a test, either."

"I've read that most things can be duplicated. What does this do to the economy?"

"You'll see. Come on—we've got a lander to catch. Economics still decree that we use launch windows."

"The Perfidisian ship came to the surface to pick me up. Why can't the *Peloros*?"

"They may have been richer than I am, I don't know. At any rate, the *Peloros* refuses to have anything to do with an atmosphere. She tells me it's a personal prejudice, but frankly I think it goes deeper than that." She grinned and took him by the arm, leading him around the curve of the ship to a vehicle bay.

NINETEEN

The city of Tokyo occupied a strip of land three hundred kilometers wide, from the Sea of Japan to the Pacific. On the Pacific coast, where Yokohama and Kawasaki had once been, were five Soleri structures, each twelve kilometers tall, surrounded by a hundred thousand hectares of city greenspace, then a vast jumble of townships, each following its own architectural plan, each with over ten million citizens. The central city was a cubic Masserat structure, twenty kilometers from base to top shuttle terminals, each vertical side interrupted by a hemispheric depression lined with thousands of apartments, a vast honeycomb dripping with people. The four corner supports, once bare and for structural purposes only, were now frosted with residential districts.

No material edifice could support such a strain so the fabric of the cube was laced with thousands of intertwined energy fields. At night, light from the field junctions turned the sides of the city into lattices of red, blue, and green stars. Their glow brightened the skies for a thousand kilometers around.

The islands of Japan supported one billion human beings. The coastal waters carried interlinked floating cities. Heat production in the larger population centers was so great that the tops of forty cities glowed a dull brown-red at night. Every fifteen minutes bursts of coherent heat from the cities were shot into space, aimed by computers to avoid the complex network of shipping in orbit above. Every so often the computers misdirected fire, and a city's waste would temporarily blind a warper ship or cook the crew of a smaller vessel.

The southern island of Kyushu was a reserve, carefully maintained by gardeners and scientists. In the cities and townships lotteries were held every day, choosing the lucky citizens who would be given permits to tour the forests and sample the uncrowded life of preindustrial Japan.

Kawashita received a permanent pass. Nestor was given a more limited pass, with a total of four years' occupancy allowed to her, to be taken in periods of any size.

The governments of Japan, China, and the Hispano-Anglo Republic—the largest nation on Earth, encompassing England, North and South America, Australia, New Zealand, and Borneo—welcomed them with special ceremonies.

"The radio temperature of the Earth is ten billion degrees Celsius," Kawashita read from his new tapas, a gift from the Hispanglo ambassador to Japan. "The total population is one hundred billion human beings. The keeping of private animals is illegal in most nations. One third of Africa is a zoo. Another third is unreclaimed wasteland from the combined effects of a misguided asteroid in 2134, and the only nuclear war, which was fought between Algeria, Libya, and Morocco in 1995. There are plans to convert this wasteland into a new African population center, with thirty Soleri structures and sixty field-reinforced Masserat structures." He put the pad down and looked outside his apartment window at the blue and purple of the horizon. Stars didn't twinkle at this altitude. The sun's brightness was grayed by polarized crystals in the glass. "Fifteen years ago a rocket bus carrying two thousand passengers hit Tokyo's central city at an altitude of nineteen kilometers. The population of Japan hit zero growth that day."

Anna was peering at a private data screen in a nook just above the dining room. Kawashita stood on the lower step of the nook and tapped her on the shoulder.

"Hm?"

"What are you looking at?"

"One of the Ring Stars went supernova forty-eight years ago. I'm looking at a lower-space transmission from the closest listening station. Want to see?"

"No, thank you. Anna, this Earth is insane."

"Crowded, yes, but I wouldn't call it insane."

"Why not?"

"Because the median income is the highest of all the human worlds. The poorest families have living allowances that would be the envy of a family on any handful of colony worlds. Franklin Wegener took the global economy and geared it to information processing, and that put Earth in a crucial position. What she couldn't have by mandate and imperialism, she took over by sheer necessity. You're visiting one of the five most important information centers in the human Galaxy—and that includes the Aighor birthworld, Myraidne, and . . . Mars? Is it Mars or the Crocerian birthworld now? Have to look it up."

"But what do they do? How do they think?"

Anna turned away from the screen. "No more wars, no more major diseases, no starvation, poverty only for those who want it, and a living environment a tiny bit better than most spacefarers put up with."

"But they've lost something."

"I'd like to know what." She returned to the screen. "Christ, what did they have around that star? I see hyperfine structures I've never heard of . . ."

"I do not know," Kawashita said, standing by the window, barely three meters from the thin, cold air of the tropopause. "Something." There was a catch in his voice. Anna swung her chair around and noticed the glitter of a tear running down his cheek. For the first time she saw Kawashita crying. She climbed out of the nook. She had never hugged him before, but she did so now without hesitation.

"I am ashamed," Kawashita said between hard sobs.

"What is it?" she asked, holding him to her.

"Where my grandparents once lived. It is covered with five kilometers of concrete and steel."

Anna wondered whether the crack-up was beginning. Half a dozen expert psychiatrists had counseled her to expect it. "Hell, Yoshio, to tell the truth, I wouldn't live on Earth for a week longer than I had to. Maybe that's what you're talking about."

"This isn't my land anymore," he said. "Not where I can search. But if what you say is true, most people are happy." He wiped his face quickly with a sleeve.

"One way or another. Happy may not be the exact word."

"So they are not like me, not like the people I knew. And I have to find answers in relation to myself. This is not the world."

"Then you'll have to find another."

"I learn day and night, and still I am ignorant. I don't have the appropriate mental conditioning for this. No matter how hard I struggle, it doesn't come naturally."

Anna squeezed him harder, as if to hold him together. "We've all known it would be difficult," she said. "Maybe we didn't really know how difficult. Perhaps we shouldn't have come back."

"Then how would I have known?" Kawashita asked. "Besides," and he backed away from her, straightening, "there are still things I must do and see."

The apartment voice announced, "Mr. Joseph Nakamura is at the door."

"Let him enter," Kawashita said, wiping his eyes quickly.

Nakamura, appointed by Independent Consolidations to chaperon them around Earth, came in wearing a smile and very little else. He was blond, with the vaguest hint of a surgically induced epicanthic fold. "Fine day out, I see," he said, walking past the window but not looking down. His eyes swept the apartment with nervous interest.

"Minus sixty degrees up here," Kawashita said.

"Sunny and fair in the tropopause. I have our schedule for today. We're due at the Kyushu visitor's center in an hour. I hear Yoshio is going to be offered a permanent residence there, on the spot of his choice. Then—"

"I'm not up for exhibition," Kawashita said. He looked imploringly at Anna. "You're my tutor, my guide. Help me out of this. I don't want to be a museum piece."

"Then," Nakamura continued, hardly skipping a beat, "we've set up a submarine tour of the Marianas trench, including a visit to the old Kraken Works. The Japanese still eat squid, you know—and the bigger they are, the more economical. After that—"

"We won't be getting that far, Mr. Nakamura, so don't bother with the rest. Yoshio doesn't appreciate the attention he's been getting, and I understand why. From here in, you can help us by serving one function only—keep our whereabouts secret."

Nakamura kept smiling. "That'd be no function at all, Anna. I'm assigned to—"

"Then your assignment is over. I can put my own people to work, and nobody will know where we are. Infact, I like that idea better. Yoshio, we're leaving the central city in a few hours—want to pack your souvenirs?"

"After my own heart," Kawashita said, heading for the next room.

"What will it be, a honeymoon?" Nakamura said jovially.

"We're not married, and we don't cohabit," Nestor said. "We're friends."

"Come on, Anna. You're known far and wide as a connoisseur of—"

"Anytime I let you finish a sentence, Mr. Nakamura, interrupt yourself for me. Voice, Mr. Nakamura would like to inspect the hallway."

"Sir," the apartment said pleasantly, "the features of central city's many corridors are famous around the Galaxy. First to be noted is the unique shifting design of the carpets, changed every hour, featuring the art of the Earth's finest—"

"Your wish," Nakamura said. "Pleasure to serve you this far. To be candid"—and his face became candid—"I think you're better off that way. More relaxing. Anytime, however, you wish to—"

"Voice!"

"—craftsmen. This way, Mr. Nakamura."

Anna sighed and returned to the screen. The apartment voice cleared a mechanical throat. "Mr. Nakamura is on his way, madam. I'm afraid there's another interruption, an insistent one."

"Who?"

"Time-and-motion planner aboard the *Peloros* wishes to speak to you."

"Jason DiNova. Put him onto the visit circuits."

"Any time limit before technical difficulties should interrupt?"

"No. Jason's one of us, usually. Thanks for your concern."

"Gracious madam. Here is Mr. DiNova."

A man appeared in the center of the room looking tired and upset. DiNova was just over a meter and a half in height, stocky but trim, with fierce eyes, a short chin, and a scalp half bald, half covered with wiry white hair. "Anna. You're not clear yet.' His delivery was rapid and husky.

"Gives me an advantage, Jason. Wait a second and it'll all come through."

"Ah. Okay." His eyes focused on her, and he looked around the room. "Fancy. But we've got important things to talk about. I gave you one month for Kawashita—is he here?"

"Packing."

"And you've gone over by two more months. You've lost two billion in revenues because of that and put two acquirable planets on USC's list. You've got to tell me what's coming up. I understand taking the USC guy under your wing on Kawashita's planet, but isn't this going a bit far?"

"Probably. Kawashita is a friend now, Jason. You know I give friends more time than I should."

"I've got a schedule for the next six weeks, and I'd like you to examine it before it goes into ship's planning."

"Transmit it and I'll look it over."

"Are you going to start a scene with this guy?"

Nestor's face hardened. "Don't push it."

"You ordered me to push it whenever necessary. I think it's necessary. Does he go with us, become part of recreation hours like the rest of the entourage, or do we—" He stopped. "Hell, I don't even want to suggest an alternative. You might take me up on it."

"Kawashita is an honored guest of the *Peloros*. He'll stay with us."

"Why?"

"Because I'm interested in what's going to happen to him, and because I like him."

"Yes, and so do I, but if I let my interests get in the way of my work, you'd have every right to restaff my billet."

"I'm glad you can't reciprocate. I have plans for Yoshio, don't worry."

"He holds a single planet, and not a very important one, as it turns out. I've had to turn down meetings with five Independent Consolidations reps—and at my guess, that means we've passed up business with a hundred planets. Anna, is this called love, or some new kind of insanity?"

Nestor turned away from DiNova's image and climbed into the screen nook. "Jason, you're getting personal."

The man held up his hands. "All in the line of duty.

Remember. Don't restaff until I start insulting you during rec time."

"I'll okay ship's planning as soon as I get it. And I'll send check-ins with my position every few hours. Hire a security team, or send one down from the ship—make them discreet. We'll probably be back by week's end, and unless you've got plans to put *Peloros* on starshine duty—"

"Nothing at the moment, but I may have to hire her out as a dance hall to pay the orbit rental."

"—unless that happens, I don't think I'll be needed for a week."

"How's he doing?" DiNova asked.

"He's got courage. He's walking on the edge of the cliff, but he's already overcome more than the psychs said was possible. Riding out culture shock, coming to terms with himself—and all the time questioning his deepest values. Think you could do that, Jason?"

"I wouldn't want to try."

"Nor I. So let me run this through its course. We won't lose anything we really need."

"What are you going to do about the Ring Stars?"

Anna pointed to the screen. "I'm keeping my eye on them. Looks like the supernova has dusted the whole area with superheavy elements. We might stake a few claims."

"No word from the Aighors, and no word on whether the disrupters are still operating."

"Keep me informed. I'm not beyond the pale, Jason. I'm still interested and aware."

"Glad to hear it. Follow your wyrd, Anna, but keep my heart and arteries in mind, all right?"

"I'll try, Jason."

"Thank you." He looked very worn, and Nestor felt a twinge of guilt. Her slightest whims could take years off a good man's working life.

"Jason, you have my love and respect. If anything goes critical, pull me up no matter what I say. And Yoshio too, of course."

"I'll do my damnedest. Out."

"Out."

A faint haze hung in the air where DiNova's image had been. The voice spoke up. "Where may I send your commodities, madam?"

"Kodiak, Alaska, and book us right behind them. Voice, you've done well by us so far. Can you get us an agent who'll be discreet and too set in his ways to care about world news?"

"I've anticipated madam. One is waiting your instructions at this moment."

"Good. Voice, have one of your programs charged to the ASNWS *Peloros*. You're a first-class design."

"My children thank you."

TWENTY

"I laid a false trail," Anna said. "We have two days left on Earth before the *Peloros* can take advantage of a conjunction. Where do you want to go?"

"I heard Nakamura say we had an appointment in Kyushu."

"It's been canceled."

"Then let's keep it."

Anna smiled. "I know why you're doing so well. You've got a devious mind."

He shook his head. "I have two places to visit there. I have read of a man I would like to meet, and a museum I would like to visit."

The surface effect ship, rented just hours before, made its leisurely hundred-knot passage with almost no sound but the whoosh of spray and music coming through speakers in the bulkhead. They sat on an upper deck, letting the sun shine on them between the shadows of high, woolen clouds, watching the blue-gray-sea and the distant haze of the Japanese coast. Just an hour before, they had passed a maritime city farm, like a giant snowflake laid gently on the sea, surrounded by thousands of submarine pens marked with brilliant orange buoys.

Now the air was cooling, and it looked like a storm was coming. Nestor handed Kawashita a pair of polarized glasses and told him to look through them. He peered up and saw a distant curtain of shimmering light marching across the sea ahead.

"Weather controls," she explained. "We're entering a planned low-pressure disturbance. I'll tell the pilot where to take us, so he can chart his course and skirt the weather.

When she returned, he said, "This ship is old. Can it stand the strain?"

"Easily. They'll sling a tarp across the upper decks, warn us we'll get wet, then go below. About the worse that can happen is we'll blow a little off course. Do you want to stay up here or go below?"

"What are you going to do?"

"I haven't felt a big blow in fifteen years. I'd like to stay."

"Then I will stay."

"Why?" Nestor asked.

Kawashita patted her hand. "In case you go overboard, I will throw a life ring."

"I mean it," she said, her face straight and serious. "We've been around each other for a long time now. Everything has gone smoothly, we always stick together, we never complain. We joke and laugh and sympathize. Why do you want to stay around me?"

"Not because you remind me of Mother, if that's what you're worried about," Kawashita said. "I could find someone else to guide me. But I'm curious about you."

"Why, because I'm famous?"

He shook his head.

"Rich and powerful?"

"Oh?" He smiled. "I didn't know that."

"I said I'm serious. Why?"

Kawashita looked uncomfortable. He took off the glasses and folded them, then swiveled back and forth in his seat, tapping the railing with one foot. "I haven't used any of the devices in the laboratories," he said. "And I haven't accepted any requests for shared quarters."

"So?"

"I think things would go badly between myself and someone from the future—my future. I'd seem childish, a savage. Japanese men are not by nature discreet. But I'm not really from the past now, am I? I've been too many people, lived too long."

Kawashita stopped swiveling his chair. "I'm curious about you because you're so hard, but you worry what happens to others. You behave like a man—"

Anna cleared her throat.

"—tough and capable, but when you cause pain, you hurt yourself. You cannot be very happy."

"I don't know about that. Why shouldn't I?"

"Because you never know why a man loves you. Or if

he loves you at all. You must look very hard, search carefully. Have you found anyone yet?"

"No," Nestor said. "Sometimes I think I have, but then . . . nothing. I have to break it off."

"I am afraid to mix, and you are afraid to trust."

"So what are we going to do?"

"I haven't been to bed—is that an obsolete phrase?—I haven't conjoined with a woman in over three years—with a real woman in more than four centuries. For a while I thought it didn't matter anymore. But around you it does matter."

Nestor winced as a drop of rain hit her face. The crew unrolled tarps and plastic roofing behind them. The first rush of cool wind made the ship's stabilizers complain. "Usually, when I'm curious, I explore. But I've been shy for some reason. Perhaps I think you're too delicate."

Kawashita laughed. "I've survived battles at sea, air crashes, sinking ships, the rise and fall of dynasties, the viciousness of an ambitious daughter and a *shogun*, not to mention four hundred years. Delicate? I don't see that."

"Then I shouldn't be afraid of you."

"Hell, no!" Kawashita almost roared. "I am still young, and there are better things to do than get blown around and soaked. Madam, you who are so much younger and more delicate than I, will you accompany me below? We have much to catch up on."

Nestor shook his hand. "I've heard that Japanese men were—"

"A base and slanderous rumor," Kawashita interrupted.

"Now you don't even know what I was going to say!"

The ship lurched as it hit the squall line, and the sudden scream of wind drowned out their laughter as they wobbled down the steps to their cabin.

Kawashita was neither as strong nor as exotic as some she had had, but there was a hint of his years in his lovemaking, a perfection of nuances which she found disarming. She relaxed with him, something she couldn't remember ever doing before. Her back and neck became almost fluid, and her jaw muscles felt so good she was afraid to talk. They held each other for an hour after, then lay apart on the old-fashioned fluid-filled bed, talking. Kawashita told her about his parents and grandparents, his brothers and sisters and cousins and what they had done in old Japan.

"I don't talk about my family much," Nestor said. "I'm not ashamed of them, or anything, but it just doesn't occur to me. After what you've gone through—battles between Taira and Minamoto, and all that—we'd probably be pretty humdrum."

"I'd like to hear," he said.

"With you, I don't mind," she said. "But you may have to prod me. I'm not used to confessions."

"I'll prod."

She looked up at the ceiling and tapped her fingers on his arm. "My grandfather pioneered fifty planets and sold their contracts to United Stars. Then he pioneered sixty more and sold *their* contracts to Hafkan Bestmerit. Hafkan Bestmerit wasn't quite the same then as it is now, because it allowed a small group of humans on its 'board,' or what served the same function. Otherwise, even then it was a consortium of alien species. It took some bloody-minded bastards to stay sane among the Crocerians and Aighors and Danvelters—and they didn't stick it out long anyway. They splintered and formed Dallat Enterprises— and that may explain why Dallat's been so long achieving respect and decorum.

"But my grandfather—Traicom Nestor—stayed away from most of the politics until he was older. He married when he was fifty, after a long free-lance career. Some people thought my grandmother, Joyaness, was a nova-baiter—in old terms, an incorrigible bitch. But that was still a time when strong women were looked on as perverse, something against nature.

"I knew her better. Joyaness took over Traicom's disorganized finances and suggested he offer himself to high office in an *economische*—which is another word, now obsolete, for consolidation. At the time, United Stars was strongly socialist and wouldn't have anything to do with entrepreneurs like Traicom, except to buy worlds from him. So Joyaness took a look at new-formed Dallat, saw great possibilities, and suggested he go with them. Dallat was more to his style.

"He was accepted into the original group of nine men and two women who had founded and splintered the consolidation. And he promptly took a second wife, Diana.

He had Joyaness's full approval. If anything, Diana was more sanguine than Joyaness. He had a financial seraglio in the making. The three of them got along famously. Joyaness and Diana were sisters by persuasion if not flesh; and besides, Diana owned a great deal of Dallat's exploratory branch.

"Traicom became head of exploration. Joyaness became adviser to contract maintenance, and Diana oversaw the design and construction of the ships. Both women had daughters, one of whom died on a difficult colony world at age ten. Both had sons. Traicom, his two wives and three children—my father included—were nearly killed during the Dallat purge years. They became leery of that and put their assets into cultural data on a folio of developing worlds. They stored the data in two exploration ships and vanished for twenty years. Their two ships were among the first to reach the Greater Magellan. My father, Donatien, married a cultural biologist four years into the journey. She was Juanita Sigrid, my mother. I was born a year and a half later.

"When we came back from the Greater Magellan, our cultural data had grown in value, just as Traicom had predicted. We were very, very rich—and we had information on things found in the Magellan, too—"

"What things?"

"Maybe I'll tell you sometime," she said, smiling, "but for the moment, let it stay a delicious mystery. United Stars was less socialist and more willing to deal, so my family established ties with them. Some day I may exercise a joining option and get support from USC—but I'm still having too much fun on my own. The family stayed independent, selling information when our funds ran low, reinvesting in data from free-lance expeditions to the Horsehead and Lesser Magellan. We doubled our assets in less than a year. Then, when we were just about ready to deal with Dallat and USC as equals, everybody went off on their own. After a tour of Earth, Traicom boarded me at the Centrum Astry's best schools. I was fifteen. I quit them when I was nineteen, on my own. We weren't nearly as rich then. Everything had gone downhill. So I took my share of the remains and formed an independent consolidation.

"By the time I was twenty-one, I had found and explored four worlds. Good ones, too. I sold their contracts to USC, since I didn't have sufficient assets to develop them on my own. Two others I sold to my grandmother, Joyaness. Her *economische* died with her—just two years ago. Father still runs an independent consolidation. We compete with each other now and then. But I haven't seen him in a long time. And so, here I am."

"How did you become rich? I mean, as rich as everybody says you are . . . it doesn't seem a few handsful of worlds would be enough."

"Two years ago I inherited Joyaness's share of the family lode. When Grandfather died the same year, I got that, too. I put a lot of it into improving the *Peloros.* Since then I've been very busy. Most of it has come in the last year. Then some auspiseers and journalists decided I was news—to be so rich so young. They set out to make me a legend. I guess they succeeded. News travels fast—even trivial stuff, as if there weren't enough important information to spread around. That's it, on a chip."

"It makes me more curious than I was," he said. "I will lay traps for you—lead you into more details."

"You can only try."

They lay quiet and listened to the noises of the ship and the high seas outside. Rain skittered on the deck above their bunk.

"I read that some Japanese study the past very closely," Kawashita said. "But I had to laugh when I saw some of their reconstructions. I can't return to that time, so I might as well leave Earth. But this man—he seems to be more thorough than the others. I will ask him a few questions, see if he fulfills the purpose his kind used to be good at."

"What is he?" Anna asked.

"A priest. After that, we will visit a museum."

TWENTY-ONE

The Kyushu Preserve was like an emerald set in marble. Not all of it was strictly preserve, however. Kagoshima was an amusement park and cultural center, which doubled as a sea protein farm. Those who water-skied on Kagoshima Bay were warned to be on the lookout for the occasional escaped Kraken or whale-bass.

Much of Kyushu was hauntingly familiar to Kawashita. The city of Moji stirred him deeply. He knew it better as Mojigaseki, which had been fortified by the Taira before their defeat in the sea battle of Dannoura. That battle had been fought in the Shimonoseki Straits, not far from Mojigaseki. Kawashita's—or Tokimasa's—future relation, Yoshitsune, had assured the power of the Minamoto by defeating the Taira decisively. But Yoshitsune's karma had gone against him, signaled perhaps by the loss of the infant emperor in the battle, and virtually as important, the loss of the Sacred Sword. Yoritomo, Japan's first universal *shogun,* had later removed his valiant younger brother from this Earth in a burst of suspicion and jealousy. Had Tokimasa's daughter figured in the plot? Perhaps, perhaps . . .

Anna plucked at his sleeve, and he broke from his reverie. She smiled and pointed to the corner where they were supposed to turn. Moji had been restored to its twelfth-century state, and the streets were filled with people dressed to fit the time. Not all of them looked Japanese. Though most were citizens, many were blond and robust, and some spoke English, Russian, and Chinese. The confusion pained Kawashita. His memories of the decades he spent as Tokimasa were muddled enough. He was relieved to be taken off the street into an immaculate wood-frame house with rice-paper walls. They removed their street shoes in an alcove and were greeted by a plain young woman, pure Japanese, who led them through a *shoji* screen into the waiting room. There she served green tea and a choice of sakis with a minimum of ceremony. This wasn't traditional but an accession to possibly ignorant visitors. Politeness was more important than ritual, and Kawashita approved of this.

They sat on cushions on the *tatami* mat floor. Anna squatted easily, sipping the *cha* and admiring the simplicity of the decor. The woman opened another screen and gave them a view of a rock garden planted with purple-blooming irises. She then bowed and left.

"This is beautiful," Anna said. "Did you live like this under the dome?"

Kawashita nodded thoughtfully. "When not otherwise engaged," he said. "I tried to keep my life as simple as possible."

From the opposite side of the room a short, heavily muscled man entered. He wore a plain black kimono and his hair was cut to a fuzz on his mahogany-brown head. He smiled and bowed deeply. "I am honored, Nestor-*san*, Kawashita-*san*. I am Ichiro Yamamura. You will please pardon the lack of proper ritual, very sorry, Kawashita-*san*, but this is to benefit Anna Nestor, who may not realize the point, no?" His eyes were pitch-black with very large pupils, and his hands were rough with hard work—a distinguishing characteristic on Earth.

Kawashita bowed and spoke only English. "By all means. No need to apologize."

"And to tell the truth, I like to relax from the masque now and then. The ritual is very enjoyable, but I'm not from your time, Kawashita-*san*, nor from the twelfth century—which, I understand, is your time also?"

Kawashita assented with a slight nod.

"Your message and reservation were met with great joy here. All of Kyushu would like a chance to meet you—both of you," he added, smiling. "I am very privileged. Of course, there will be no charge."

"I won't hear of it," Kawashita responded quickly. "This is your work, your business. We'll pay the regular fee."

"Ah, in this day it is polite to say such things, but let me reach back to a time when refusing such an offer was the height of boorishness, no? Very sorry, but this will be—as some Americans have said—on the house."

Kawashita smiled and graciously agreed.

"Now what may I do to help you?" Yamamura asked.

"You may help me to find my place in this world," Kawashita said. "Of all the people here, you are perhaps the best for answering such a request."

"*So desu*," Yamamura said. "That is so, or maybe so. But I am many things now—still however, not a psychologist. I design religions for many kinds of people or lead them to find their own harmonies. I'm not just a Buddhist, please understand."

"Understood," Kawashita said. "I don't seek a religion for myself, simply answers about where I will best fit in."

"How do you see your universe now?" Yamamura asked. Anna shifted on her pillow and concentrated on the tea.

"I'm not sure."

"How did you see it before this marvelous life of yours reached the point of . . . crossing over?"

"As a vast, complete whole, ruled by the laws of karma, occasionally influenced by the"—he hesitated and lifted a hand to speed expression—"Spirit which occupies all."

"You believed in reincarnation?"

Kawashita nodded. "As a match passes a flame to another match, or candle to candle. The passing of an impulse."

"Then you were much more sophisticated then many of your contemporaries, even in the twentieth century. Did you believe in the accretion of karma from past lives?"

"Yes."

"Then there must have been some belief in you of continuation of personal characteristics from life to life."

"No, I don't think so," Kawashita said. "Karma was passed on regardless of the connection."

"Do you believe in karma now?"

Kawashita shook his head. "I don't know. Not very much."

Yamamura turned to Anna. "I'm sure you'll find a tour of the gardens very enjoyable. My wife, Aiko, will show you around. Yoshio and I have many things to discuss, and we must use Japanese for best results, I think, very sorry! Please." The woman who had shown them in reappeared, bowed, and motioned for Anna to follow her.

"What does Yamamura-*san* do to help his clients?" Anna asked as they followed a curving flagstone walkway through the exquisite gardens.

Aiko smiled as if at some secret joke and shook her head. "I don't know for sure," she answered in very good English. "I'm more dedicated to playing my role than he is. When we meet, he plays his role deeply—a priest of long ago. When we are apart, he does most of his work, and I don't know what it is very much. He builds, I think, worlds of faith for many people, many besides the Japanese. Is this what your companion needs?"

"I don't know," Anna said. "Maybe another Japanese can help him."

"Perhaps."

They ate a light lunch of pickled vegetables and raw fish on a small frame porch overlooking an artificial waterfall. Geese wandered through the shrubbery, and Anna was delighted to feed them bits of fish and special biscuits. She avoided more than just tasting the fish herself, but admitted it wasn't bad. "I'm used to much more processed foods," she said.

"Of course. It is very ungracious of me, but I have a question about Yoshio-*san*. May I beg your pardon and ask it?"

"Certainly," Anna said.

"I find myself caught between times, now and then, like a ghost stepping out of a silkscreen painting. This is part of my role, and I accept it. But for him it must be a thousand times more difficult. Is he doing well?"

"Overall, he's doing very well," Anna said.

"That is fine to hear. Japanese are very hardy people, and in some ways the people of Yoshio's time were used to being between two worlds."

"How's that?"

"Allow me to tell you a fairy story, still very popular. It is the story of Taro Urashima. May I?"

Anna nodded. The woman's whole manner was foreign and absolutely delightful. She had never felt so at peace as she did in Aiko's company.

"Yoshio is very much like Rip van Winkle, but even more like the fisher-boy Urashima Taro—our way of placing names. Fifteen hundred years ago, Taro was fishing when he captured a turtle, sacred to the sea. So he let the turtle go. To reward him, the Dragon King of the Sea sent his daughter, who was very beautiful, and she took Taro back with her to the palace of her father. The Dragon King's daughter became Taro's flower-wife. For a time he was quite happy, but one day he desired to return to his home and visit those he had left behind. His bride begged him not to go, but he was resolute. So she gave him a box and tearfully instructed him to go if he must, but to always carry the box with him, and never open it.

"When he returned to his fishing village of Suminoye, he recognized no one. Buildings and forests had changed. He came across an old man and asked him where the Urashima family was. In answer, the old man led him to a crumbling, almost forgotten graveyard. There, Taro saw the gravemarkers of his father and mother—and his own marker, for he had been supposed to have died at sea, four centuries ago.

"Taro became suspicious that a trick was being played on him. He opened the box given to him by the Sea God's daughter, and a white mist escaped, like the clouds swept from the skies of a million clear summer days. Before he had time for regrets or second thoughts, his hair grayed, his skin wrinkled, his teeth fell out, and he collapsed in a pile of dust.

"To this day, that dust may be found in the concrete and stone of Japan's new realm. The ghost of Urashima Taro—and the gentle sin of his doubt—haunt us even now, for we live between two worlds, just as he does. Just as Yoshio. In Yoshio's time, adjustments were very hard. And if he searches for answers, perhaps he should know that, remember. His people were like Taro in a new world, and they could not know how to behave properly."

Anna looked down at her hands, close to weeping. She couldn't tell Yoshio this, not now. But it seemed so clear and compelling. Perhaps too much so. She glanced back at Aiko.

"And if you doubt that Yoshio is like Urashima Taro, then remember . . . He vanished from a great steel ship four hundred years ago, and was not seen to this day. And what was the name of that ship?"

Anna thought. "The *Hiryu*," she said.

"Yes. That means 'Heaven-bound Dragon.'"

Anna nodded.

"Now. May I explain to you about these gardens? My husband does not like me to meddle, so I return to my duty, proper and honored." She smiled at Anna and took her hand.

Two hours later, filled with peace and a better appreciation for the patterns in the garden, Anna was led back to the main part of the house and shown into the chamber where Yamamura and Kawashita were still sitting. Aiko left.

Between the two men were three swords, two long killing swords and a short blade. They looked very old, not by being decrepit or fragile, but by the exquisite workmanship. The handle of the short sword was an artfully arranged lobster carapace, each segment acting as a finger grip. Yamamura bowed as she sat beside them. Kawashita seemed lost in thought.

"We have reached some decisions, I think," Yamamura said. "Yoshio has decided against suicide, and I concur with him—though that may be because I am not truly accurate in my replication of the past."

"Thank God for that," Anna said, looking at the short sword with more respect.

"And," Kawashita said, taking a deep breath, "we cannot stay here. There's no place for me here, as I thought. Even Kyushu isn't Japan as I knew it. This is a place for historians and tourists—for games, not simple living."

"I am not the one to answer Kawashita's questions," Yamamura said, his eyes far away on the rock garden. "No one on Earth can answer his questions for him. But he has asked about the Perfidisians and what sort of beings they are."

"Yes," Kawashita said.

"I think . . ." Yamamura's mouth tightened. "If they are gods, they are lackey gods, servants."

"What do you mean?" Anna asked.

Yamamura shook his head and broke the spell, grinning. "Pardon my foolishness," he said. "What can I know about such things? You see, I was right in not charging you, because I have answered nothing and solved nothing, only perhaps verified what was already suspected."

"What do you mean about the Perfidisians?" Anna persisted.

"A guess, based on intuition, if you will. From my work. Again, I am proud to have served in my small way." He smiled again, and it was obviously time for them to leave.

Yoshio was quiet as they took ground transportation to their next stop. As they approached the bay, Anna saw a huge series of hangars stretched along the shore.

"What are those?" she asked.

"We are going to see them. Be patient."

"Christ," Anna said. "I may not have much patience left in me. Why are Japanese so mysterious?"

"Inscrutable?" he said, and she grinned.

"We've been through that already."

"We like to give surprises," he said. "We are like children that way."

"Oh."

The entrance was a tall archway, at least two hundred years old. Blowers hummed faintly in the huge hangars, but otherwise they were quiet, almost empty. Anna thought that whatever they held wasn't very popular any more.

"It's a maritime museum," she said, reading a display at the opening to the first hangar. She walked ahead of Yoshio and stopped, astonished.

The hangar contained a ship. It had to be just under three hundred meters long, mounted on a complex series of risers and supports. The hull was scored and scraped and badly mangled in places—huge holes with steel projecting inward, revealing twisted decks, passageways, engines. The propellor shafts were bent and the propellors themselves covered with a crusty growth.

She looked at more displays projected in the open air around the ship. "This is an aircraft carrier," she said, reading quickly. "Japanese. It's not yours, is it?" She looked at him sharply, suddenly worried.

"No. This is Admiral Nomura's flagship, *Akagi*. She was built on a battleship hull, not very stable in heavy seas. But she did well enough. The airplanes which bombed Pearl Harbor flew from this ship."

The huge hangar was filled with a slightly acrid smell which Anna couldn't quite identify. She guessed it was a mix of the smell of the sea and the ship, burned and scored and decayed.

"I read in the guidebook," Kawashita said. "These ships were raised two centuries ago, during a period of intense interest in Japanese military history. Great expense, great effort. Opening the tomb of the sea."

They took a moving walkway through the first hangar, into the second, which contained a large battleship in even worse condition. Scaffolding hinted at half-hearted restoration work. "This is the *Yamato*," Kawashita said. "She was sunk at the end of the Second World War. At one time, before his death, she was the flagship of Admiral Yamamoto. It was here that he heard about our defeat at Midway, and became sick with fear and rage."

The third hangar contained a collection of small ships and submarines. They passed through quickly to the fourth.

"Another aircraft carrier," Anna said. It was smaller than the *Akagi*. Not much restoration had been completed. The hull was broken into three sections, held together by special lift fields. The island superstructure was on the port side, and a huge chunk of skeletal metal had been lifted up by an explosion on the forward flight deck.

"*This* is my ship," Yoshio said.

Anna held his hand tightly. His throat was taut and his arm was almost rigid as iron.

"They bring my ship back, and now you bring me back. We are not very much like we were, last time we saw each other." He took her over to a bronze plaque under the looming propellors, darkened with age, on which hundreds of names were inscribed in Japanese characters. Two other plaques on each side translated in Cyrillic and Roman letters.

Anna read the Roman letters, found a sub-heading, "Pilots," and went down the alphabetical list.

She found what she was looking for. "Kawashita, Yoshio, Sub-Lieutenant."

"These are the dead," he said.

On the hovercraft, Yoshio was lost in thought, chin held in his fingertips, frowning slightly. Anna sat beside him for an hour before breaking the silence.

"Where to now?"

"I'd like to go to many places. Can we arrange that?"

"I think so. DiNova will bitch, but—"

"Do you trust me?"

Anna held a knuckle to her teeth. "No, not completely. I haven't been around you long enough."

"Do you want to take a chance?"

She felt her heart jump. "On what?"

"On an old pet monkey, suddenly become a lover?"

"You're cruel."

"Well?"

"What kind of a chance?"

"The whole shot," Yoshio said. "Whatever the ceremonies are now."

"You're picking a hell of a time to ask," Anna said, her voice cracking.

"Then this is a hell of a time for an answer."

She had never been inclined to spend a long time making decisions. She weighed everything but found no rational arguments one way or the other. "Buddha and Lords," she breathed. "I'm supposed to love him—you, the man. I'm supposed to—"

"Do you?"

"All?"

"The whole shot."

"Except financial," she mused. "You don't need that. You're a planetholder."

"Okay."

"You're a fool, Yoshio."

"Then you're a bigger one, no?"

"Where, and when?"

"On the ship, when we return, soon."

"You won't believe this," she said, her voice breaking. "You're the first who's ever asked. And you're the only one I thought I could say yes to."

"Then?"

"Yes!" She ran away from him, down the stairs to the covered lounge. Yoshio sat in the starlit dark, nodding his head, whistling an old popular Japanese song.

TWENTY-TWO

"Goddamm it, let's get some order on this ship!" Anna stormed across the bridge, glaring at the officer of the deck in orbit. "Social occasions aren't worth the loss in time."

"Congratulations, madam," the ODIO said, smiling at her over his shoulder.

"Leave this ship for a few weeks and everything falls apart." She ordered her chair out of its nook and sat in it imperiously, lifting her hand to warn away an attending sphere. "Mister Oliphant," she said to the ODIO, "call Mister Kondrashef to the bridge. We are about to do unspeakable things to space-time."

Oliphant stepped back from the bridge monitors and stood with his hands clasped behind him. He was officially relieved of duty until another port of call was made. Kiril Kondrashef appeared on the bridge in a uniform slightly fancier than the occasion called for. Nestor looked him over with a withering stare.

"In celebration, madam," he explained.

"Of what? Having something to do for a change?"

"Of your impending marriage."

"What cause do you have to celebrate? Think I'll soften in my conjugal bliss?"

"A contented captain is a good captain, so the legends say."

"Tell me if you notice any difference. Request permission to leave orbit, and make damned certain a waste beam doesn't cook our sensors. I'll expect you to dodge."

"Request made," Kondrashef said, watching the automatic sequencer. All orbit organization was handled through computers. "Permission granted. Rental charges halted."

"I have a series of worlds plotted on my duty tapas,"

she said. "I expect to orbit around the first objective in about seventy hours."

"How many objectives?" Kondrashef asked.

"At least twenty. We're looking for a good place to honeymoon."

"Kyushu wasn't good enough?"

"Terrestrials don't think the way we do, Kiril. Yoshio and I are seeking peace and quiet on far, sparsely peopled worlds. A romantic quest."

"Very well. We'll enter first warp in ten hours."

"Fine. Yeoman," she addressed the hovering sphere, "notify DiNova that I'm canceling all business dealings which can't be handled by ship-to-ship or deep-space communications. He'll select the best dealings for me, to be delivered to my cabin."

"When's the happy day?" Kiril asked.

"We'll be married on Bayley's Ochoneuf," Nestor said. "If you do your job right, in seventy-two hours."

"Do you remember what it was like, sleeping through the warp?" Anna asked.

Kawashita shook his head. "I'll be ready for this one," he said. "As long as it isn't too strong."

"One of the hazards of the trade, like getting seasick on a boat."

"I was seasick for two weeks on my first deployment," Kawashita said.

"The effects are minor on a well-tuned ship. Without warp it would take us a thousand years to get where we're going, and ten times the fuel." Kawashita nodded but didn't seem to listen closely. He watched Anna's body in the light of the cabin modifier, like a ghost, her shadows brownish-warm from the floor's afterglow. As she turned, the air fluoresced around her, leaving a series of heat-images.

"You like?" she asked.

"Beautiful."

"Me or the modifiers?"

"Women haven't changed much in four centuries. Still full of vanities."

"Ha! I saw you trying on new hairstyles in the mirror. Vanity, thy name is Methuselah."

"When I read through the libraries under the dome, there were so many books fearful of technology," he said. "Afraid computers would take over mankind—"

"They did," Anna said. "On Myriadne, three hundred years ago. And maybe one or two times since—mechanical shutdowns, balky systems; that sort of thing. We design around them now."

"Or that technology would leave us neck deep in poisonous muck. They hardly ever mentioned a time when something like a modifier could turn every motion into art.

Or when ships could bring the treasures of other civilizations to all corners of the human Galaxy, without wars—"

"The wars exist," Anna said. "But they're chiefly economic, or psychological."

"So now I'm filled with optimism," he said. "I've lived long enough to see."

"You didn't like Earth, though," Anna said, bringing her face down to him and pointing a finger at his chest.

"In my time there was only three percent of the population Earth has now, but more than half lived miserable lives. Who am I to complain? I'll go somewhere else to live."

"Don't think it's all rosy, Yoshio," Anna cautioned, lying beside him. "You've only sampled the surface. And you've had all the facilities of the rich to fall back on. Lots of people are still unhappy. Most."

"Then they're fools. They're well-fed, educated, have the resources of a galaxy's information within a few minutes' reach—"

"On Earth perhaps. But when you get to the fringes, the new colonies, life is much harder—harder than it needs to be. There are still tyrannies and wars and torture. I've seen some of it. Earth is old and stable now, but very few of its citizens can experience new things directly. They're locked into their lives by the security they've built up. On some colony worlds people can experience a thousand different lives—and face the consequences. Adventure and novelty are hellish things most of the time. For every asset, there's an equal or greater number of debits."

"What are your debits?" Kawashita asked.

"Estrangement from my family. Loneliness—even now, though you fill a big gap. But one future husband isn't enough. How many friends do I really have? A few, subject to the vicissitudes of employment. A few in the entourage, people who accept me as I am, without trying to get more from me. But none I can call close, not like a friend I had when I was a girl—"

DiNova's voice broke in. "Anna, my regrets. This is an emergency. We have twenty minutes until warp sequencing. The Aighors have officially denied all knowledge of activity in the Ring Stars."

Anna sat up on the bed. "How many ships are headed there now?"

"Who can count them all? Five hundred, a thousand."

"Can we beat them?"

"If we use our geodesic buildup and blow half our fuel."

"We won't find any more around the Ring Stars. Tell Kiril to get us there, and use three eighths if he absolutely has to. We can't afford to gamble with the rest. Our allowance is inflexible." She looked at Kawashita, her face wreathed in a smile.

"What's happening?"

"If the Aighors deny any responsibility for the Ring Stars, we aren't limited by treaties. We can mine as much information as we want."

"What will we do when we get there?"

"If we get there ahead of everybody else, we'll put some special equipment to work. If you're going to be my husband, you'll have to learn some family secrets. Think you're ready for them?"

"If you don't expect full understanding."

"Hell, I don't ask that of myself."

"The Waunters will be there?"

"Not before us. Their ship will run a long, long time, but it won't push through higher spaces nearly as fast as *Peloros*. Hell, Yoshio—we're riding a hard, gemlike flame!"

Kawashita had never seen Anna like this. She paced back and forth across the cabin, talking of things he knew little or nothing about—pinching the ship's hole to increase spatial evaporation, analyzing the Ring Stars for charm and cohesion effects after years in a probability-altered space—and so on, for the quarter hour until warp sequencing. A bell chimed on the ship's intercoms.

"Be at peace, mates," Kondrashef advised in somber tones. "We're riding into hell again. God save your bloody souls."

Kawashita shivered involuntarily. The modifiers were automatically cut, and room lights became bright. Anna lay next to him with her head on his shoulder. "You're trembling," she said.

"It was the same before I received inoculations as a child. Waiting and not knowing what it would feel like."

The lights dimmed to orange. His nerves tingled.

"Warp status," the intercom said.

Kawashita shut his eyes, then found he preferred them

open. The dark was too pregnant. "We'll force the *Peloros* pretty near her limits," Nestor said. "Squeeze the hole until it gives up three eighths of its mass. That will deepen our plunge. The farther we go from status geometry, the more energy we have to expend to keep ourselves together. It's a vicious circle. So we play our cards and stay within the limits of the hand already dealt—we have no idea what we'll pick off the table when we get there. It's not pleasant being stranded. The cost of a Combine or USC expedition to rescue us could break my fortune into little tiny pieces. Are you ready for a few family secrets?"

"I don't know. I can't seem to think straight."

"The simple ones, then. What we found on Grandfather's trip to the Great Magellan."

TWENTY-FOUR

Kawashita lay in the dark, watching Anna sleep, watching the play of lights on the ceiling—designed to soothe warping passengers—and thinking about his fiancée's family. He closed his eyes and tried to picture his first fiancée—an eighteen-year-old girl from Nagasaki, with smooth, pale skin and eyes like a flinching doe's. But there were only bits and pieces left. At any rate, there was no comparison. Anna, if less beautiful to a Japanese, was certainly more dynamic and suited to him now.

But what price her energy? Born in the Greater Magellan, tens of thousands of parsecs from the nearest human outpost, she'd been raised among her family and the crews of the exploratory ships. Her mother, Juanita Sigrid, a cultural biologist hired by Anna's grandfather, had fit into the unusual family as well as could be expected. Anna had assumed some of her traits: empathy, a certain cynical view of things, which masked uncertainty, and a touch of bitterness. For when the family broke up, Anna's father and mother went separate ways, and Juanita Sigrid got the worst of everybody's opinions. Traicom Nestor, Anna's grandfather, regarded her as a traitor to the son he didn't quite trust himself. When she remarried, she broke all ties with the past—including her daughter.

Anna's father was now head of an independent consolidation. He seldom communicated with Anna, but she felt a great deal of affection for him. Her mother she felt less regard for.

Behind them all, like the background of a complex painting, was the Greater Magellan. Juanita Sigrid had found her job cut out for her.

On the near side of the cloud of stars they'd discovered an abandoned artifact—the largest structure ever found. It interconnected three stars a parsec distant from each other and contained the mass of seven rocky planets. Like an old spiderweb strung across the light-years, spun from carbon and silicon and coated with a thin film of metal, it had been abandoned long before. Without extensive energy to hold it together, it had separated into a fine cloud of debris. But that cloud still retained a haunting shape—a cupped disk with three triangular wings, aimed at the center of the Milky Way—or where the center had been forty million years before. Two worlds in the area had once supported life, and there was ample evidence that beings on both worlds had supported each other in the project. They'd apparently never developed warp technology. Their greatest effort had been spent on easing their loneliness, trying to communicate with unknown beings, for unknown reasons.

Beneath the shallow seas of one world, in ruins scattered by geological forces, the expedition managed to piece together glimpses from the distant past. Then, in a near miraculous find, they rescued a few metal tetrahedrons from deep trenches that had once been the coast of a continent. Stored in the atoms of the tetrahedrons were the histories of both civilizations.

The Nestors selectively sold the information for a dozen years after their return.

But the financial angle didn't interest Kawashita. He wondered how the two species had felt, locked in by the agonizingly slow means of traveling between their three stars. He wondered if they'd succeeded. If they had, where did they go? And if they hadn't, did they die a natural death or commit suicide?

He couldn't sleep. His head was filled with visions. No matter how hard he tried, he couldn't dispel the notion that all of space and time was haunted, that every centimeter of every parsec, in all directions, was filled with *kami*, watching and listening.

And at this moment, stretched through some higher space that was making his deepest thoughts scatter back and forth like rain in a storm, they were traveling to see the creations of still more *kami*.

Everyone was foolish not to see it. Everything was wrapped in plan and deceit. He couldn't begin to guess where he fit in. but he knew his role was far from minor. And he had failed. Once he knew why, he had two choices—the same choices he projected onto the builders of the Web as they faced their success or failure. He had lived a very long time. Not even his love for Anna could color his decision.

For that reason he stayed very quiet now and put on the masks of knowledge, acculturation, matrimony. He hoped they would come off easily when the time came.

TWENTY-FIVE

Ships went into the Ring Stars and, if they survived the outer fields, were swept out of existence just beyond. Sometimes, light-years away, like the cast-out debris of a carnivore's lunch, bits and pieces of them would return. Sometimes the emergency signal beacons were still working. Ships outside the fields would pick up the signals, intercept the debris, and find nightmares, things from other universes mixed with the fragments of the lost ships.

Ostriches with large heads, gelatinous blobs with chunks of crystalline seawater adhering to their bristled skin. And worse. Ship fragments that were alive. Everything had been mixed into a cosmic grab bag, and samples had been plucked out.

The Aighors didn't deny that they were responsible, in the beginning. The theory of the moment was that they had developed probability disrupters, weapons that could exchange mass-for-mass with world-lines slightly askew from status geometry.

Then the supernova spread its shell of light out through the fields, through the anomalies, following with a tag-along shell of particles. The flower bloomed in deep space, deadly and timeless.

The pyrotechnics had ended long ago. An expanding nebula of gas and hard radiation surrounded the remnant of the Alpha star.

Leaving higher spaces within the small solar system of the Delta star, the *Peloros* immediately began absorbing data. Beneath a faintly silvered energy shield, robots normally deployed for cleaning the warp nodes were installing new equipment in the sensor clusters of the outer hull.

Anna supervised everything with obvious enjoyment. The first few hours out of warp, she was in constant motion, giving orders and making decisions. Jason DiNova followed a few steps behind, grinning. This was the Nestor he was used to working for. Domesticity seemed as ill suited to her as a wool comforter on a star.

Then, as if on cue, Nestor withdrew from the activity and sat down in an unused corner of the cargo bay, chin in hand, brows together, deep in concentration. Two yeoman spheres hovered nearby. DiNova stood to one side, leaning against a bulkhead.

"All right," she said. "Bring the chapel furniture down from inner C, manufacture a few runners of white linen, clone some flowers in Special Projects. I've recorded plans and designs in my notes. Look them up. I want it all down here in six hours. Send invitations to all ship's personnel, and special dispensations to watchholders. The *Peloros* can run without supervision for a few hours, right?" She looked at DiNova. He nodded.

"Fine. Pardon me for a moment," she said. "I have some apologies to make."

Kawashita was in her cabin, exercising with four light metal poles he'd borrowed from Materials Dispensary. She watched him set to a pattern of moving abstract hologram images, wiping them away with intricate swings. When the exercise was over, she interrupted.

"I'm sorry," she said. Kawashita looked up. "For running off like that. But I can't promise I'll mend my ways."

"So? We both took chances, no?"

"But I know you've still got quite a bit of masculine pride. I shouldn't go out of my way to tread on it."

"You have work to do, obligations. Any discomfort they cause me is minimal."

"What are we going to do when you find a place you want to settle?"

"I know what I will do but not what you'll do."

"Most of this is in my blood. So I tell myself, anyway. Without it I might be a different person. But—"

"You shouldn't give it up, then."

"I was going to say, I need some time to decide what I'm going to do, how I'm going to be. I don't want to traipse across the Galaxy after every will-o'-the-wisp of potential profit—not for the rest of my life. I saw what that did to my family. After this I want to put it away for a while, try something else." She sat in a desk field. "Do you believe me?"

"Not completely," he said.

"Willing to take a risk?"

"Yes."

"We're both idiots, you know," she said.

"You, who take risks every day of your life—risks that can decide the future of everything you've done—you worry about one small chance?"

"I'm a coward. I have soft underbellies that can be ripped open. I've never let anyone get at them before. When I commit myself to you, you'll have all the road maps to them, and a set of claws."

He put the poles down and held out his arms. She stood and came to him. She was sweating and her back was stiff. "If I knew I had any soft parts left, I'd tell you where they are," he said. "Fair exchange. But I don't know where they are myself. I have only one goal, and there's no reason anyone would try to set me on a different course—not even you. We'll give each other more freedom, not less, if only because we provide points of rest for each other—sea anchors in a storm."

She pulled back from him and smiled. "Talk about May-December marriages," she said.

"Is everything ready?"

"Will be shortly. Kondrashef has agreed to be your best man. And DiNova will give me away, which is symbolic, I suppose. I can hear him worrying about all the projects we'll pass up after I'm married. I have friends in the entourage who'll act as maids of honor, flower girls, and the like."

"I'm not familiar with this kind of wedding."

"Nor am I, believe me. But you told me to design it as I saw fit."

"I've never been much at remembering lines."

"It'll be simple. A short walk, a ceremony, witnessings."

"And a working honeymoon. It does seem crowded."

Anna sighed. "I couldn't pass this one by. Too much at stake."

"To the Japanese, a wedding means a great deal."

"It means a lot to me, too. Still, I see . . . it would have been nice to have time to ourselves right away." She put her hands on her hips and shook her head. "Are we getting off to a bad start?"

"You were worried about knowing what you want. Do

you really want this?" His face betrayed nothing. His tone was reasonable, and Nestor couldn't tell if he was expressing dissatisfaction, or if she was merely fighting her own guilt. "Yes. I do."

He smiled. "The only thing I ask is that you know what you want. I'm flexible. I can do what I wish almost anywhere."

"I wish I knew what you really thought" she said. "You seem too damned reasonable."

"Your risk," he said, smiling.

"One part of me says you should stand up and make me back the hell out of the Ring Stars. The other says you're letting me follow my wyrd, like I was some kind of summer thunderstorm, useless to interfere with. I don't know which I prefer."

"What you'll find here interests me," he said. "If the *kami* who call themselves Aighors didn't have anything to do with these stars, then who did?"

"You think the Perfidisians had something to do with it?" She paused, her lips held tightly together. "Damn you. You're taunting me. What the hell *do* you want? Tell me straight, or I'll cancel the whole thing!"

"Are you angry?"

"Goddamn right I'm angry! You're playing me like a fish on a line! Tell me straight!"

Kawashita folded his hands behind his back and took a relaxed, at-ease position. "I've seen you before when you're angry. You lose all reason. So—don't interrupt—listen carefully. You don't control me. Your circumstances don't control me. I decide for myself and base those decisions on things you cannot understand—experiences I haven't told you or anyone else about. I can return to my own world and live well enough. I don't depend on you for anything but the dubious luxury of traveling all over the Galaxy. It's a matter of interest, not necessity. It isn't for myself that I criticize condensing the ceremony, or holding it out here, where its ghost is rooted to nothing, where no one can ever pinpoint its place with any certainty. It's what you will think later, how you'll feel about our bonds. I marry you to stay married. I don't consider it a pact of convenience. I learned that a variety of bed partners doesn't satisfy me. I don't want to be alone any more than I have to be. If you wish to wander far from me, at any time, then don't marry me."

"That isn't what you said a few minutes ago."

"So love makes me inconsistent."

"I don't know what I want to do."

"Then don't marry me. I know what I want to do—have to do. If I am the anchor, and you're a far-straying ship on a thin chain, we might as well not marry."

"No," Anna said. "It would be a travesty."

"I might have done that once, if I'd married during the war. I might have left a wife at home and fought far at sea, perhaps died. But I didn't. That philosophy has stayed with me."

"We shouldn't get married?"

It was Kawashita's turn to be irritated. He turned away from her and squared his shoulders. "I want to."

"So do I. But I'm not sure I can live up to everything. Shall we compromise?"

"Do we even know the limits within which we can compromise?"

"I think I can set them out. Fidelity."

"If that is what you want," Kawashita said.

"I want it. I'll consult you on all business journeys—all journeys, of any kind. But we can't make a fixed rule about them. It just wouldn't work."

"No."

"I don't know how much I have to wander, just to stay sane. But I will let you help me decide." She held him around his shoulders, laying her head onto the back of his neck. "We've both contradicted ourselves. I guess neither of us knows how to work this kind of thing out. Being reasonable isn't enough."

"We won't make lasting decisions now. We'll work things out as we go along."

"Wherever I go, I want you with me."

Kawashita laughed. "We're both crazy. You more than I. You have everything you want, and you want more—you want to be satisfied with less. I'm willing to put up with anything but not willing to be separated from you." He turned around in her arms, rolling her chin on his shoulder until she was looking up at him. "The thought of doing without you scares me. I don't know who else I'd turn to."

"That's not fair to you," Anna murmured.

"So is there anything different about us? We make a contract, just as billions of humans have done for thousands of years—we feel afraid for each other, afraid of living without each other, which is the height of immaturity. Like two adolescents."

"I'm not that far from adolescence," Nestor said. "Not compared to you."

"So? Look at me. My body hasn't changed since I was twenty-five years old. My needs haven't changed. I've never felt like an old man, even when all those around me thought I was a patriarch."

"You don't conjoin like an old man."

"Until now, I've been mating with ghosts. Shadow-fucking. I've been asleep four centuries—and now that I'm about to marry you, my life starts up again."

"I want to please you."

"Now that we've said these things, the wedding is just a formality, a party for the rest of the ship, no?"

"I've never been much for formalities, myself."

"It's simple. A short walk, the ceremony, witnessings," Kawashita said.

Nestor tapped her chin on his chest and grinned. "Wish us luck?"

"No wine, for a toast?"

"At the flick of a wrist," Nestor said. She ordered wine and it rose up from the food table in two long-stemmed glasses. "Vintage," she said. "Not manufactured. Tapped from kegs in the cargo bays. I bought some on Earth before we left, for the wedding. Let's sample it before we force it on the guests."

They drank to each other. "Christ," Anna said, laughing as she wiped her lips. "It's green. I'll have to run it through the processor anyway."

TWENTY-SIX

Direct excerpt from the tapas records of Yoshio Kawashita. Translated from the Japanese by Language Program (Trevor)—1360-C Twentieth.

Married. Almost trivial, four hundred and some years old, recording a marriage. Married before, seven times, but to people who didn't exist. I know the institution, but through the distortions imposed by divine spirits.

Married to Anna Sigrid Nestor, strong, loving, fragile. Like jumping off a cliff. Beneath the dome, I was never nervous about being married, any more than an actor on stage. What was I committing myself to? But now I can choose to let my time run short—to die. A marriage can take up a substantial portion of the rest of my life—perhaps all of it. For Anna it was a nervous time, too. Between us we sweated lakes. Slurred our speech. Laughed at our mistakes. Some cried with Anna. Some laughed with me when I delivered my lines in suddenly broken English, as though I'd forgotten

Married in the cargo bay, by an interdenominational minister. License witnessed by the *Peloros* Testament as legal counsel for the ship, under supervision of three human lawyers; these signed our license. Belong to no country; our legal obligations are minimal. Things are much simpler this way. Any children—natural or, more common, *ex-utero*—are automatically entitled to a percentage of our holdings equal to the number of children, divided into half of the estate, subject to legal alterations by our personal Testament programs. Are other ramifications from common law, but have no place here.

After the ceremony and hours of celebration, Anna took me aside and suggested it was time to begin the honeymoon.

And so we did.

The next wake-period, the *Peloros* announced its presence in the Delta system of the Ring Stars. Anna assigned Kawashita as a second officer aboard a lander, and Kondrashef acquainted him with exploration procedures.

Call signals from four hundred other ships were logged in the first week. Among them was her father's flagship. Arrangements for a meeting were made, and the two warper ships docked in stellar orbit. Visitors, luxury supplies, and news not available through general transmissions were exchanged. Then, without announcement or ceremony, Donatien Nestor came aboard the *Peloros*. Anna met him at the makeshift visitor's station in the lander bay.

He was a tall, lean man, with powerful features that reminded Kawashita of some of the armor masks he had worn—a sharp, hooked nose, eyes inclined upwards at the sides, thin lips which, in a smile, always seemed to have the advantage of you. He gave Anna a peremptory hug, congratulated her on being among the first to arrive, then turned to Kawashita.

"Is this our long-lived new family member?" His voice was mellow, mid-ranged, pleasant. He held his hand out, and Kawashita clasped it firmly. Donatien's grip was light and unassuming. The Japanese bowed, and he returned the bow, but with a diffident look to one side. "You have quite a history. Unfortunate it was interrupted."

"I've lived a great deal longer because of that," Kawashita said.

"Anna." Donatien hugged his daughter again, still with some reserve, as if unsure exactly what to do.

"I've missed you, Father," she said.

"We've missed you, too. Much work was done, however. I hear you're doing well."

"Very well. Yoshio and I think we can afford to take a

few years off after we're done here. We plan to travel around for a while—as tourists."

"Never done that, myself," Donatien said. "Probably never wanted to. Kawashita-*san*, how do you get along with my strong-willed offspring?"

"Very well," he said.

"Remarkable. Not a bit of accent. You seem to be adjusting."

"I've had a long time to prepare."

"So you did. Are there refreshments, a place to relax for my party? Anna, this is my domestic partner, Julia Horsten"—a tall, thin woman, almost skeletal around the wrists and ankles but smoothly filling out around hips and breasts—"and your half brother, Marcus." The boy was about ten years old, sandy-haired, and husky. He smiled politely.

"You flew airplanes?" Marcus asked.

Kawashita nodded. "A long time ago."

"Sunk aircraft carriers?" the boy pursued.

"More sinned against than sinning," he answered, shaking his head.

"The social side is what I'm here for," Julia said, peering around the lander bay like an exceptionally dignified deer. "But I'm sure Donatien wants to discuss partnerships and pacts."

"Partly. Anna, is your sensory equipment as good as I think it is?"

"Father, we're on different pledge-sheets now."

"So we are. Is she breaking you in, Yoshio, or are you on a different pledge-sheet, too?"

"We are communal, I believe."

"Totally," Anna said. "But Yoshio has his own fortune. He doesn't rely on me . . ." She interrupted herself, unsure the implication had even been made. Then she called DiNova from the shrouded sensor equipment waiting to be loaded onto the lander and introduced him to the family. "Jason knows more about the ship than I do, and he's probably dying to talk business, but he's even more interested in escorting a beautiful lady and fine young brother around the *Peloros*. Correct?"

DiNova nodded with studied enthusiasm. Julia looked at him with a faint air of disdain but took his proffered hand and told Marcus to come with them.

"Very good," Donatien said. "I assume you have the special sensors ready—you'd be foolish not to use them, and you're no fool. Daughter, this isn't going to be as important a find as some people think. Do you have that feeling?"

Anna cocked her head in query.

"I'll give you some free information. None of the matter in the three systems we've scanned has been altered in the least. The supernova cloud appears to have an unusual hyperfine structure, but there doesn't seem to be any correlation between that and the probability distortion."

"If we're exchanging data, Father, I don't have anything to offer in return."

"Not at all. What I'm saying is, the evidence will have to be purely artifactual. Nothing subtle seems to have changed."

"Except the Alpha star itself."

They began to walk around the perimeter of the lander bay. Anna kept edging them away from the shrouded equipment packages. "Purely a natural event. Despite what the Aighors say, I think they had something to do with it."

"They didn't," Kawashita said.

"Oh?" Donatien looked at him with a challenging smile. "What do you think, Kawashita-*san*?"

"The Aighors are brilliant, if Anna's library is accurate, but they aren't secretive in the least. Their claims about the Ring Stars show nothing but their willingness to take advantage of a mystery."

"True," Donatien said. "They're not known for human honesty. Their idea of truth varies considerably from ours."

"I think the Perfidisians were responsible."

Donatien nodded. "Either way, artifacts will be the only things left behind."

"There won't be any artifacts of value if they were Perfidisians," Kawashita said.

"You're correct there, of course, but the *if* exists. Anna apparently thought the risk was worth it. I do, too. So the chase is on?"

"I was hoping we could relax for a while," Anna said, "without discussing business."

"Sorry," Donatein said. "I'll leave Marcus and Julia here for the socializing. I have to be back as soon as possible."

"No," Anna said, smiling coldly. "No spies, no hindrances, Father. They leave when you do."

"They're lambs," he said. "Total innocents."

Anna laughed. "Different pledge-sheets, Donatien. You're welcome to stay awhile, all of you. If you want."

"The race is on. There are sixteen chunks of rock in this system, fourteen in Gamma, three in Epsilon, and one remaining in Alpha. I'll see every one as soon as possible and sweep them as thoroughly as I can."

"Luck to you, then," Anna said.

"Are you up to her, lad?" Donatien asked, looking over his shoulder at Kawashita. He turned and held out his hand.

"Someday you will ask whether she was up to me," Kawashita said without expression, shaking his hand with a matched light pressure.

"Perhaps. If Mr. DiNova will roust Julia and Marcus, we'll be off. Thanks for the time."

"Not at all," Anna said. "Relatives, even if on different sheets."

"Certainly."

They left as quickly as they'd come, and with as little ceremony. Kawashita followed Anna to her cabin. She paced aimlessly for a few minutes, then allowed a few tears. "He wouldn't even stay an extra hour," she said.

"He's a strong man."

"Oh, I could stand it if he were just a strong man, a good businessman. But I have this cursed, old-fashioned notion that families are supposed to be loyal to each other, not to pledge-sheets."

"You mentioned them first," Kawashita said.

"Because I know my father. Donatien would try to seduce an angel if he thought it would increase a voyage's profit margin. Well, I think he's on the wrong track, Yoshio. I still love him, but I'm going to teach him a lesson. We're not looking at chunks of rock. I'm going to examine the old forbidden zone and see what there is to see."

"Wrecks," he said. "Scattered debris."

"Exactly. Whatever happened here, it spent its force outward, and it was long gone by the time Alpha blew." She rang up DiNova and delivered her instructions. "Turn all sensors to the old boundaries, and give us a short warp out there. We're going to gamble a bit."

There were thirty physicists aboard the *Peloros*, each with a specialty, all the specialties adding up to a well-integrated whole. When the new sensors were deployed, they began a patient search for things much finer than needles in haystacks, or individual sand grains on a beach—the remains of spacecraft intercepted by the Ring Stars probability disrupters.

They listened for the dim emanations of atoms that had been violently shunted between closely similar universes. The sphere of disruption had had a radius of twenty-five light-years from the orbital center of the Alpha and Beta components; since the frequency of remains increased inversely with the distance from the center, the best concentrations would be found inward from that, if any still existed.

Nothing was found in the first week. Yoshio tried to comprehend the scale of the search, calculating on his tapas the volume to be covered. Since the physicists considered it unlikely that any debris would have been released within a radius of twenty light-years, the volume was reduced—only about 2.7×10^{43} cubic kilometers. He shook his head and grimaced.

In the second week, further reducing the search volume by following the complex curves of warp exit points for vehicles from major known civilizations, they found a three-ton mass of slightly radioactive scrap metal. There was no clear indication of its source, and though it had been through a disruption, it could just as well have been an asteroid used for target practice. Nevertheless it was taken aboard, examined, and stored.

At the end of the first month everyone was tired and the search was slowing. Reports from ships in the first three systems being studied indicated nothing had been found there, either. DiNova, looking at the energy budget and schedules for possible projects in other areas, made his first suggestion that the *Peloros* should return to regular duty. Anna ignored him.

Kawashita finished his training on the lander and began taking instruction from DiNova on Nestor's personal economics. This was harder for him than most of the technical and scientific material. Despite his work with early Japanese economics under the dome, as adviser to the *Shogun* Yoritomo, he had little acquaintance with the art. DiNova instructed him well but somewhat impatiently. Neither was very impressed with the other.

Kawashita then took a turn at standing low-activity bridge watches. His first fitness reports, compiled by the ship's second officer and delivered to Kondrashef, gave him high marks. The work reminded him of the long nights on the *Hiryu* when he had stood on the bridge with the flight officer, waiting for dawn. In deep space there was no dawn, unless he counted the distant torch of the Alpha component in one of its last shows of glory, now twenty years old.

In the sixth week a tiny chunk of debris was located. To confirm the trace, all the ship's equipment was shut down for ten minutes and the sensors were subjected to a rigorous cool-down. The trace remained.

"It measures at a kilogram mass, two hundred thousand kilometers from us," the leader of the search team reported when Anna came to the bridge. "The trace is very weak, and it seems to be fluctuating, declining at the moment. We may not be able to find it if we move closer—"

"Or even if we stay here," Anna said. "Keep track and send a lander after it. Coordinate—have we got equipment mounted on a lander? What are you using?"

"Virtual particle disruption with subsequent production of—"

"Which lander can match it?"

"Four."

"If we can't find it within five days, tell Mr. DiNova he can lay in a course for Bayley's Ochoneuf." She sighed. "I'm tired. A new bride shouldn't be so tired, should she?"

The leader grinned. "Depends."

"Think about putting yourself on report for flippancy, and let me know what you decide," Anna said, turning to leave the bridge.

"Yes, ma'am."

The lander was loaded with retrieval robots and launched from the bay an hour later. Slowly, like an animal stalking prey much smaller than itself, the lander nudged itself across the distance, deploying its finest sensors. The robots went out into the silent dark, special dampers muting their electrical interference.

Kondrashef and DiNova joined the team leader on the ship's bridge. "We've got it," he said when the indicators came on. "One and a half kilograms. They're bringing it back."

Most of the ship's crew and at least a third of the entourage gathered in the cargo bay as the retrieval robot was wheeled in on a cart. It produced a transparent package like a proud mother.

"Looks like a piece of something larger," Kondrashef said, touching the capsule with one finger. "The edges look abraded, perhaps by contact with other debris in a small cloud."

"Ship's store memory has a source, sir," an attending sphere said.

"Oh?" Anna said. "Where does ship's store think it comes from?"

"It recognizes the fragment as part of an outdated STW-67 unit, madam. A ship's toilet, weightless utility. Definitely terrestrial in origin and manufactured prior to 2300."

"Ship's toilet," Anna said, peering through the packaging. "It doesn't make our voyage, does it?"

"Unless we can trace its ship," DiNova said wearily.

"Twenty thousand units were made," the sphere said. "Essentially identical, no records detailed enough to allow identification."

"Jason, I'm ready to go. We've had our share of snipe hunting."

"Gladly."

"You're going to be snippy too, hm? I suppose I deserve it. I wonder what Father is thinking now? I doubt he's found anything."

Kawashita came to the bridge. "I can feel them here," he said. "I *know* they were here."

"Doing what?" Kondrashef asked. "Playing cosmic checkers with our spaceships?"

"Play's as good a motive as any," Anna said. "Maybe they're just youngsters playing hide-and-seek, and we're it."

Kawashita shook his head. "Very old children."

"Never growing up, never having work to do, never creating a rational pattern of behavior? Sounds good to me," Anna said. "I'll log that over a big 'don't know.' Our first theory designed to fit the lack of facts. Congratulate us. And send congratulations to Father, Kiril." She took Yoshio's arm. "I wasn't kidding about a sabbatical. Jason's going to wipe the schedule now. We're going to have a real honeymoon, just you and I, in about two dozen places very far from here. I don't want to turn into another Donatien."

Kawashita visited the observation sphere six times. Each time, he approached it with trepidation. He could never predict the full flavor of his reaction.

In the sphere, slouched in comfortable weightlessness, he looked the stars over with a frown.

For the sixth time, he requested the same lecture. The sphere chimed and began.

"The distances between stars are lost when ships use higher spaces. An awful immensity is replaced by a short disorientation of the nerves. It is an economic exchange, but one which can give a false perspective. When travel is judged by the consumption of energy, when the longest voyage usually attempted is three months, and economics rules the sway of a wandering heart, space is civilized, some say, and the adventure is gone . . ."

Kawashita was barely listening. His mind was elsewhere. He was well-fed, well-loved, busy enough. Most of the time, his driving questions were in the background, where they didn't occupy his full attention. The centuries under the dome were memories that seemed to have little effect. But a pervasive malaise still churned in him. Under the dome his limits had been broad, practically infinite. But here, suddenly mortal, everything he did was final. He felt his scale in an indirect way—not as a matter of size but as a matter of accounts. One side of the account book was filled with the daily minutiae of life, the other with the number of things he'd be allowed to do before death closed in. The number in the second column was vanishingly small compared to the actions required for perfect knowledge. So perfect knowledge was a perilous way to wisdom.

". . . But nothing is further from the truth. Between warps, all a traveler has to do is take a short glide down

an access tube to the observation sphere, ten meters outside the ship. The ship seems motionless in a black universe pricked with stars. Weightless, the traveler can
position himself in the middle of the sphere, his back to
the access tube, and feel as if his eyes are the only things
for endless trillions of kilometers. The darkness is profound. After a few minutes, the mind relaxes into
blankness . . ."

Anna's people took the path of perfect knowledge as a
matter of course, rushing here and there to build a complete picture they could never see. But another way was
just as futile, even perilous—the way of abstracting and
symbolizing. Soon enough, the language of abstraction
would swallow its devotee and leave his thoughts mired.

Then there was the way of contemplation. As he now
understood this time-honored path, contemplation led to a
suspension of certain mental programs and the enhance-
ment of others, and with this came the mastery of mental
life. But throughout history, isolation had been necessary
for the thorough contemplator. Kawashita enjoyed his life
too much for that.

". . . After a few minutes, the mind relaxes into
blankness. The patterns of the stars seem very important a
while later, and the craziest notions about religion and philosophy pass through the mind—childish questions: How
did God place the stars where they were? Why do they
suggest animals, people, or faces? That passes. The next
phase is cold terror, and the traveler has to grip himself—
clasp his arms with both hands, lift his knees up to see if
they're still present—and force himself to stay. There's no
horizon, no circle of familiar objects, no orientation of
any kind. The distances come back as a reminder, and
though the eye doesn't really believe them, some part of
the mind—perhaps the part most superstitious about written records—does believe . . ."

Kawashita squinted at the stars, knowing he was seeing
much less than there was to see. The tide of sadness rose
until his eyes filled with tears. He couldn't even pray any
more—the faces of the spirits were too far gone, too confused with the faces of simulacra; the *kami* had taken new
forms, not to be prayed to; God (or Goddess) waited im-
placable, silent. He wasn't searching for them.

". . . Some will try to calculate how many human

bodies, stretched end to end, would reach from the ship to the nearest star. Or, at a brisk walk, how many lifetimes it would take to traverse a sidewalk magically extending from here to *there*. That passes. Numbness takes its turn . . ."

Then what was he searching for? However much he loved Anna, he couldn't begin to find it in her. Her life was dictated by immediate problems, practical solutions. But his love for her was the only thing he could fully, deeply believe was real. Everything else was a dream—starships and distant worlds, divine kidnappers and historical fantasies beneath a glass dome. Touching the hole of probabilities. Plucking debris out of space—a toilet! He smiled. It was one vast comedy, a shadow-show.

He was looking for—(a deeper frown).

For—(clenched fists).

". . . It may all end in giggling and child-like behavior. That's a bad sign. The regression may continue until the traveler simply closes his eyes. Then the sphere administers a mild shock, hustles him back to the body of the ship, and recommends a few hours of exercise and conversation. Few ever forget the experience. Some wish to have it erased, or its terror will haunt them for years after. Some reflect upon it as they would upon a religious experience. Others are unaffected, too blind, unimaginative or numb to pay it any attention. They look at the stars with less curiosity than an animal, convinced the universe is produced within them and exists for them alone."

He was looking for the way to an easeful end, a fine end, full of dignity, obligations fulfilled. He wouldn't find that way until he knew why he refused to commit suicide. According to all his tradition and training, he was a prime candidate for self-destruction. He had failed to reroute history, out of a weakness he still didn't understand—and he had inflicted suffering on myriad ghosts. Four centuries ago, he had failed to join his honored leaders in *seppuku* on the bridge of the *Hiryu*. He had failed to kill himself on hearing of Japan's defeat and the renunciation by the emperor.

He had sidestepped every basic belief he had ever held. The shadowplay had surrounded him completely. He had no choice now—he had to flow with it and let it point out his new direction.

"Entering higher spares in half an hour," the voice warned. "This sphere will close in ten minutes."

He twisted around and grasped the handrails in the tunnel.

TWENTY-NINE

"Colonies in space, colonies on all kinds of planets, free states, consolidation worlds, worlds yet to buy their independence by paying off consolidation loans . . . we can even skim by forbidden worlds, where intelligent life exists or will exist in the foreseeable future—and don't think *that* isn't a controversial distinction! Take your pick. An atlas of seventy thousand worlds. I can take four years' fuel allotment in advance, and if we combine business with pleasure every five or six worlds, DiNova says we won't go broke. Half the entourage wants off before the trip begins, but ten thousand others have applied."

"Long trips?" Kawashita asked. "How far can we go?"

"End to end, theoretically, but the atlas covers only about one percent of the galaxy. Anything else is exploratory, and we'd need to change our trip description. I think you'll be satisfied to see a couple of dozen known worlds." Anna smiled. "Besides, if we go exploratory, I can't guarantee I won't get enthusiastic again."

"Are you sure this trip will be useful to you?"

"Yes. There's nothing like seeing a place firsthand. I can suggest a few places where we can think things over in complete privacy—not just planets, but O'Neill colonies, eggworlds, asteromos."

"Soon?"

"Three days. DiNova is down at the Centrum licensing center now. In three days we'll leave Myriadne, leave everything behind."

"If we're agreed."

"We're agreed," Anna said. "I feel better now than I have in five years. Sometimes I get so used to being hagridden that the hag steps down and I miss her. But not now."

"To Bayley's Ochoneuf first?"

"I don't know how much more honeymoon I can take."

"Strong woman. You'll survive."

THIRTY

*Bayley's Ochoneuf; Lament; Potter's Field;
Santa Tsubaraya; Death's Vineyard; Iolanthe;
Ithaca; Orb Vecchio; Orb Nuova; Star's Lee;
Phoenix; Sleep; Catter Van Sees; Angel
Rookery; Dirac; Farther; Old Mao; Quantico;
Perspect; Black Pool; Plurabelle; Gautama;
Gift-of-Isis; God-Does-Battle; Veronike . . .*

God-Does-Battle was being terraformed; city builder
Robert Kahn was designing palatial organic cities for the
Judaeo-Christians and Moslems who had contracted the
world, determined to bring heaven down to solid ground,
far from the unfaithful.

Dirac was a bleak world, circling a supernovaed star at
one end of the Pafloshwa Rift. Anna picked up a chunk of
silicon doped with five superheavy elements, which she
later turned into several pieces of jewelry.

On Sleep, a thickly misted world renowned for its
floating forests, they swam in the living Omphalos Sea, letting the oils of the hundred-kilometer creature soak into
their skins, and the hallucinogenic pollen carry them into
dreams.

On Gift-of-Isis they watched a sunrise from the tallest
volcano in the Galaxy. It was a triple sunrise, on cue,
which happens once in a millennium.

On Plurabelle, a world of twenty thousand rivers, they
journeyed for a week up and down tributaries, through tor-
tuous canyons etched from rock, breathing oxygen gener-
ated at a terraforming station at Ninety North.

None of them were satisfactory to Kawashita. They
were beautiful, soothing, even heavenly—but on none of

them could he find any trace of what he was looking for.

The *kami* had never been to them, had never left their mark.

There was only one place he could go.

THIRTY-ONE

The Perfidisian planet hadn't changed appreciably. Weather patterns were more regular, the air was thicker from the outgassing of fresh volcanic vents in the southern hemisphere, and clouds were more obvious.

"You're sure," Anna said, half inquiring.

"I'm sure."

"Back to the scene of the crime."

"Back to quiet."

"The dome is still there. We can outfit it with a suitable environment, build a good home. Stay for a few years."

Kawashita took her hand and pressed it softly. "You sound tired."

"A little. I'll relax for a while—it's your game now."

"What will DiNova do?"

"He'll stand in my place. He's disgusted, but he'll do it. Two years shot to hell—for him—already, a few more won't bother him appreciably. My empire is large enough to go on for a long time without me. It may not grow as fast, or do as many spectacular things, but it'll survive. And should someone sweep it out from under me, I can build it back in twenty or thirty years."

"You sound willing to try it."

"A challenge is a challenge. But if I thought there was much chance of it happening. I wouldn't be here now." She lay down in front of him in the observation sphere. "I'm enjoying my own soul-searching. I don't worry about being another Donatien anymore—I don't use the sleep inducers as much. I see people more clearly. You've taught me a lot."

"It was there before I came," Kawashita said. "It will remain after I'm gone."

Anna frowned. "What do you mean by that?"

"I won't choose any more life than I'm due."

"You're going to abstain?"

He nodded. "There's still plenty of time left, but when it's over, I see no reason to continue my long-running show."

"I'm not sure I even know what it means to grow old and die," Anna said. "I'd hate to make a decision, not knowing."

"Growing old and dying isn't difficult. It's knowing there's no choice in the matter that's hard. A choice has been given to me, by men I'll never have a chance to thank . . . and I politely turn it down."

Anna held out a hand to encompass stars. "How long will we live together, then?"

"As long as we can. We haven't killed each other yet."

"Any other man, I think I'd fight with him at least once a week. Bad fights, nasty. But you take fights out of me. DiNova doesn't think that's good. The mellowing of Anna Nestor—bad for business. But having more control should console him."

"You trust him?"

"I trust no one, Husband—save you, and even there I have an intellectual byway set aside for doubts. You know that."

"I don't ask trust," Kawashita said. "Only your presence when I wish to touch someone warm. Speak to someone intelligent. Be silent with someone I love."

Anna looked down at the Perfidisian planet. "I think everything we need for the dome is on the *Peloros*. How elegant should it be?"

"Simple, comfortable."

"Are we going back to nature?"

"Perhaps for a hobby. A sun under the dome—we can renovate the soil, which is probably pure minerals now—recirculate the water, and draw what more we need from artesian sources. We'll do well."

"I think so," Anna said. "Time to read, plan, create little things." She mock-grimaced. "I might go crazy, all that tranquility."

"You might."

"But probably not."

Kawashita grinned and bowed as best he could in free-fall. "We'll see."

THIRTY-TWO

Elvox saw the old Aighor ship and visibly flinched. The pursuit ship's first mate looked aside from their instruments and raised an eyebrow.

"Dead stop to us, sir," he said.

Elvox nodded. "I know the ship."

"Yessir—Third Aighor, isn't it?"

"I know who owns it. Run a check on Alae and Oomalo Waunter and see if they're in the employ of anyone we know."

It was their duty to keep a watch on the ships that tried to illegally enter the Ring Stars area. United Stars was trying to keep the area closed, with the cooperation of Dallat and Hafkan Bestmerit, until everyone was satisfied there was nothing important to find. The Waunters' ship had almost made it through the thinly spread sensor nets.

They hadn't tried to run once spotted and hailed. Now Elvox's pursuit ship was closing rapidly, like a flea near a dog.

"Their equipment answers for them, sir," said the duty watch officer. "They won't speak personally. They accept a boarding request."

"Any explanation about what they're doing here?"

"No, sir, but it's implied. They're down and out. Most of the independents trying to break through are indigent."

Elvox nodded. He had almost managed to forget. Now it was all coming back. He had spent a year's lonely, dull duty overseeing experiments on Precipice 5, trying to redeem himself after the Perfidisian fiasco; he had succeeded and was now working his way through ranks, almost back to where he had started. There had been no overt disapproval—just the unexplained pass-overs for promotion.

"Find the best entrance, and have Davis dial an appropriate fitting. We'll board after sanitation checks."

"Yessir," the first mate said.

Elvox went to the research room to prepare a brief on the boarding. They'd have to search the ship from end to end. That would take a couple of days, with officers stationed on the ship until they were cleared—if they were cleared. Usually the independents found nothing of value.

He wondered why the Waunters were desperate, if they were. His old twinge of guilt returned. He could be responsible—

"We've got a fitting, sir. Edging up," the first mate reported.

The interior of the old ship was in good condition. Unlike many independents, the Waunters had kept their vessel in repair. There were no unusual microorganisms to deal with.

Elvox's team of three, including himself, boarded five hours after linking. They crossed a narrow bridge over the sea-tanks, following their charts and the scant directions given by computer voices, and headed toward the forward living quarters.

"I've seen old Aighor ships in projections," the first mate said, "but this is something else."

"They're impressive," Elvox said tersely.

The Waunters waited for them on the bridge, standing by human-form chairs, dressed in formal attire. Elvox deployed his men to begin the search.

"We regret you've inadvertently entered forbidden space," he said, following the polite ritual. "United Stars will reimburse you for any inconvenience. This action is sanctioned by the Centrum."

Oomalo Waunter nodded and smiled wanly.

"You're the officer that was on our planet," Alae said, looking him over coldly.

"Yes, ma'am."

"Have things gone well for you since?" she asked.

"Well enough."

"Not so well for us." She shrugged. "That was a turning point. Now we free-lance listen, survey. No commissions. But we have enough to listen comfortably for a couple of centuries."

Elvox didn't contradict her.

"Something will show up," she finished, turning away from him.

He kept his silence, though the pressure was building up. He conducted his men through the first day of examination, then slept aboard the linked pursuit ship.

The next morning he talked to Oomalo.

"I don't think you're doing as well as your wife says."

"Well enough," Waunter said, his voice neither denying or assenting.

"This ship's an archaeological curiosity, you know. You could sell her and settle on a comfortable estate someplace, perhaps even Myriadne."

"I'm not through cataloging and investigating. Lots of research left to do. Besides, Alae prefers the employment. We'd go insane on a planet."

"You've heard about Nestor and Kawashita," Elvox said, his voice faltering.

"No," Waunter said. "Don't pay attention to communications if they don't concern business."

Elvox nodded. The next day's examination turned up nothing, and everything but the most difficult recesses were checked. Elvox decided he trusted the Waunters.

"I feel a certain camaraderie with them," he told the first mate. "I think they're honest enough we can take them at their word."

"Sir, we were told to scrub any suspicious ship until it gleamed—"

"That's not always practical. Let's clear her and send them on their way."

The young officer nodded reluctantly. Something had changed in the CO since they'd seen the Aighor ship, but he couldn't say exactly what. A loss of impetus, perhaps.

Elvox went aboard the old ship for one last time to tell the Waunters they'd be free soon. He sat next to them in the human-form chairs on the alien bridge, watching the ancient lights gleam steadily, folding and unfolding his hands.

"I have something of a confession to make," he said. "I lost an important part of me on the Perfidisian planet. My self-respect. I didn't tell you something which I thought could be important."

Alae looked at him without apparent interest, but Oomalo smiled his old, wan smile. "Yes?"

"Nestor and Kawashita, they're married now. Living on the planet, in the dome. You know I was involved with her for a while."

Alae made no move, but Oomalo nodded.

"Her—their—marriage shook me considerably. Until I figured out their motivation."

"You mean, why she didn't go with you."

"No . . . not exactly." He tried to find the right way to say what he needed to say. Confession was such an awkward, painful means. "I spent a year working off the mistakes I made on that planet. Very unpleasant duty. I had a lot of time to think."

Alae stared at the green bulkhead to her left, blinking.

"They fooled all of us," Elvox said. "And the Centrum."

"We're very tired," Alae said. "Finish your check and let us go."

"You don't seem to be catching what I'm saying. They must have found something on the planet, something they don't want anyone to know about yet. Especially you."

When Alae looked at him this time, her eyes were steady and frozen gray. "We don't care about that anymore. Our luck has run out. We didn't even want to come here, but there was nothing left. Leave us be."

"They had an orgy, you know, after they were married. They went to two dozen planets, trying to find something for the Japanese. He never could find it. It was like they were trying to waste time until they felt more comfortable about doing whatever they planned to do. Or perhaps they were running away from themselves, until they got their courage back again."

"You are saying she would never have preferred him over you," Oomalo said, still smiling. "Unless she was well motivated."

"No," Elvox said, lying. "I don't care about that now. Don't you even want to claim what's due to you?"

"Nothing's due," Oomalo said. "Go, please."

"Everything's due!" Elvox said loudly. Oomalo frowned at his tone of voice.

"Your men have finished the inspection. They have no more business here."

"She married the Japanese to control him because she found something valuable. Together they conspired to keep it a secret so you wouldn't get your share. They want it all. And if she's willing to be secretive over so small a share, it must be a huge find—monumental. Enough to make even ten percent—"

"I don't ever want to see that planet again," Alae said softly. "I don't ever want to see these stars again. We're leaving now. Nothing but disappointment for five years. We don't need any more."

"What are you talking about?" Oomalo asked, as if coming out of a trance. "When did they marry?"

"Just after the decision. Do you know that you get everything if you prove they're holding out on you? Everything! The whole world, and all rights to what they've found."

"That planet was searched from pole to pole. There wasn't anything on it."

"How do we know that? The Perfidisians were obviously far advanced from us—how do we know what covering devices they might have used? I think Nestor stumbled on something important. If you don't look into it, you're insane."

Oomalo assumed the same level, burnt-out gaze as Alae. "Go," he said. "Take your crew and go."

Elvox was shaking when he left the ship. He was also smiling, though he didn't know it. He was too mad to talk to anyone for several minutes, but he'd just let an ugly monster off his back, something he'd carried for years. Now it was on somebody else.

It made him feel *fine* when he thought about it afterward. The injustice had been revealed to those who could do something about it. The Waunters had the legal right to call for an investigation. They could subpoena all of Nestor's records. It would cause her so much trouble, and he would be behind it all.

The ships separated.

THIRTY-THREE

Record of Yoshio Kawashita.

Building our house. A sun hangs at the upper center of our dome. The powdery hills carry grass and bushes and trees again—real this time. Rain falls at unpredictable intervals. The air is cool, vivid, changeable. Anna designs the rooms, which will be made in the Japanese style of my day. I study all that is known about nonhuman beings. We have purchased a huge library of select source material for my work. Here, I can feel the weight of my past lives, and the eyes of those who watched me, every instant, who watched all I did, and recorded it perhaps, and studied me as I now try to study them. Anna maintains they were not Gods—not even *kami*—but I wait for my own conclusions.

The dome is broad enough to have its own kind of weather, a playfulness which contradicts the environment machines. We may, if we wish, have a few animals—birds, insects. They wait to be cloned or grown from eggs. A luxury of terrestrial life waits in one box, more than we could ever need, but most human colonies have such a box, Anna says. It's the germ plasm of Earth, insured against loss by its presence on thousands of worlds. Perhaps we'll find such a box from another world, left behind by beings long dead. This world? No. I think not! (*Laughter.*) That would be too much to hope for. But elsewhere.

I take walks outside the dome at least once a week, surveying the plains but mostly looking and trying to feel for the missing things. At one time there must have been buildings, streets, perhaps vehicles—and Perfidisians. Sometimes Anna goes with me. We have a small cart which we use for longer trips, and a larger one which hasn't been used yet. In time we will cover a fair portion of the planet, place instruments at various points, and study its long-term behavior. Anna thinks we'll find very little of interest. She's probably right. But it serves as a distraction while I work on other problems.

Reading histories of many races and beings now, starting with my own kind. Aighor literature—most of the works that have been translated—Crocerian saga-histories. With electronic amplification, I can read a book of a hundred thousand words in twenty minutes, from a tapas. Still not fast enough. My head swims with dissociated facts. Lifetimes to process them all! So I am more selective now. I go back to source documents, earliest records, experience tapas when possible.

Of great interest at the moment is the period of first contacts, when two species acknowledged awareness of each other and began to set up relationships. For humans most such contacts occurred between 2035 and 2145. The politics and cultural changes of this period are fascinating.

Each day my love for Anna grows. She is still strong, independent, but we touch whenever we can. She enjoys being stroked, like a cat. She feels some embarrassment about this, but it comes so naturally the embarrassment is an afterthought. Sometimes she will try to avoid contact, but we always come together again to touch, compare our thoughts, reenergize. All of my past life is like a shadow compared to this. *Memento mori*—it cannot go on! Not forever. What will we feel when one or the other is gone? Unimaginable.

A week ago we took the small cart out on one of the (to her) monotonous journeys. She grew bored early. After suggesting we turn around before dark, which we didn't, she became silent. In the dark, the cart's roof-mounted lights shining across featureless concrete, we felt more alone than we had between the stars. Here was isolation at its most extreme—just ourselves, ten thousand kilometers of planet under our feet, and a few machines. She said she was afraid we'd lose our souls here but couldn't explain why. The hair on my neck raised and the dark was filled with ghosts. She began to cry. Humans have long since learned that some residue of living things persists after death, as a record of organized particles moving in personal spaces. Why not with the Perfidisians? By the time we reached the dome, we were both terrified. It took us several hours to calm down. She was angry with me for two days after.

But the Perfidisians were too thorough to leave ghosts behind. So what do I look for, when I go from point to barren point on the plains?

For that one overlooked item. No living being is perfect. Perhaps some individual Perfidisian forgot one tiny artifact. the equivalent of a nut or bolt, too minor to be detected by the Centrum and USC instruments. Anything. And while I look, I work, try to recall . . . What is that key I know exists, but which can't be remembered?

Anna is patient. She may last me out.

The *Peloros* has been gone for a month. It will take another four months to complete its missions and return to check up on us.

THIRTY-FOUR

Oomalo Waunter took away the sheet of paper from the bulkhead, leaning against a foam pad on the scaffolding. If there was the faintest hint of a seam, he'd find it. He was convinced the ship had secret hiding places. The conviction wasn't entirely rational—the Crocerians would almost certainly have found any hidden artifacts of value. But it was something to do. While he did it, he worried.

Since the seizure by the USC ship, Alae had brooded and done very little work. They'd left the Ring Stars and set up a deep-space orbit around galactic center while they considered where to go next. Perhaps that was what she was brooding about.

He took a graphite block and marked an X on the bulkhead to indicate how far he'd searched. When he shined a light from below, the X would reflect the glare and he could tell where to move the scaffold. He'd covered a tenth of the ship this way.

His allotted work for the wake-period done, he went to the sea-tanks, scattering his clothes along the way. Under the ceiling's strip sunlight—the inner perimeter of the ship's hull—he swam for kilometers, circumnavigating the tanks. The water was faintly slippery from some reaction with the metal bottom, but he was used to that. The ineradicable smell of iodine didn't bother him either. The Aighors had kept this artificial ocean stocked with several varieties of dangerous aquatic life, to "play" with on long voyages—mainly to keep fit and maintain social order. Dozens of ship's commanders had been chosen through combat in the tanks. Now they were quiet, except for the slap of waves on the far bulkheads and the sounds of his splashing.

Alae sat in the oblong booth which looked down across the port warp node generators. The old transparent metal had taken on a beautiful green tint across the millennia. Below, even when dormant, the generators which started the chain reactions of spacial shifting were surrounded by spikes of red fluorescence.

A half-broken tapas pad sat on her lap. It was good only for writing with a scriber and erasing with a finger. She had had it since childhood, and it served her as a kind of doodle pad. Written on its screen now were the words, "Baubles, toys, blue skies."

She had bought all the information she could about Anna Sigrid Nestor. She had studied the woman again and again during the judgment, covertly glancing at her, measuring her. What the USC loytnant had said about Nestor and Kawashita made sense. Nestor had planned, schemed, hidden, won. They—Alae and Oomalo, most deserving—had lost. The Centrum, as always, had ruled against independents. Glamor over labor and discovery. Power over—

She put the pad aside slowly and backed out of the booth. Without the subtle presence of her body's energy field, the sensitive spikes on the generators cooled to a deep, steady blue.

Oomalo was on his second lap when he heard Alae calling his name. "Waunter!"

"What?" He stopped swimming and lifted his head out of the water.

"We're going." She walked along the edge of the tanks. He swam in place with slow, regular strokes. "Where are we going?" he asked.

"To claim our property."

"How?"

"I don't know. But we're going."

Kawashita removed a chart from a plastic pouch and unrolled it for Anna. The hot bricks in a hibachi beneath the table kept their feet warm in the cold room, but little else. They were wrapped in several layers of clothing, but Anna was still chilly and not very attentive.

"We've covered these paths so far," he said. "Together, look at the patterns."

"So? Straight lines, curves, all the normal ways a vehicle runs."

"I'm not so sure," he said. "I've numbered the times we went certain ways. Some paths have been covered a dozen times, with variations of only a few meters."

"So?"

"I don't know. I thought maybe you could suggest something. After all, you were born into a more complex world." That had become a standing joke between them. Anna ignored it and said in a stage whisper, "I don't understand why we should freeze to death when we have a perfectly good environmental system. All we have to do is turn it up."

"I think better when I'm cold."

"I don't," she said. "Can't think at all. Maybe I could decipher your squiggles if it was warm."

"We can find warmth within ourselves," Kawashita said, rolling the paper. "Just concentrate on your—"

"I'm no good at meditating," Anna said. "Not as good as you are, anyway. And I'm getting tired of all this pretense. Why give up the comforts of home? And don't dodge the question—I'm getting irritated."

Kawashita nodded and slipped his feet from under the table. "I am trying to reproduce a situation," he said. "It must have been ten years ago. I had a dream."

"About what?"

"I'm not sure now. I was so involved in the illusions that I thought it was a simple nightmare. Just after we came back, it occurred to me there was more to the dream than fear. But I cannot remember details."

Anna laughed. "So you're going to nudge your memory with a bit of tea cake? Search for times lost?"

"I don't understand."

"I never finished the book, but some French author from your time wrote about incredibly detailed memories conjured up by the taste of a tea cake."

He shrugged. "The cold helps. It was in a situation like this that I ate breakfast, ten years ago, after the nightmare. It was winter outside, and I warmed my legs with an urn of hot bricks under a table. And I did something that related to the dream . . . but I'm not sure what."

"Wrote it down? Talked it over with someone?"

"No. It wouldn't have made sense to them."

Anna swung her legs out of the pit and stood up. "Well, this experiment is at an end, unless you want me to live in another part of the dome. Jog your memory some other way. If you want, we'll order a memory analyzer."

"Yes, I thought about that, but the brochures said such devices are very bad at retrieving dream memory. When the mind wants a dream forgotten, the process is pretty thorough."

"The mind, or your hosts," Anna said.

"Yes. It was something about my situation." He frowned. "I think . . . wait. I know! I was a great king, in a magnificent palace, watching a huge spiritual hand scrawl something on a stone wall with a fingernail made of fire. But what did it write?"

"Read the Bible."

"I don't understand."

" 'You have been weighed in the balance, and found wanting,' or something to that effect. An old biblical tale."

Kawashita looked at her with brows lifted, mouth open slightly, eyes showing prominent whites. "Yes," he whispered. He scurried off, robe shustling behind him, to another room in the house.

"Anna the muse," she said to herself. She reached into a fold of her robe and brought out a remote switch. "Let's get this place heated. And clear the hibachi out. Bring back the usual furniture."

"Yes, madam," the voice replied.

Kawashita scribed busily on the surface of his tapas pad. The memory extension units—containing all the libraries he thought would prove useful—rested in their cases next to his sleeping pad. A meter away was Anna's sleep-field, a luxury she had refused to give up.

The dome followed a twenty-four-hour cycle. Judging from the brightness of the artificial sun, and the color of the sky projection, it was late afternoon. Anna left Kawashita in their bedroom and walked among the bare shoots of trees and bushes planted around the house. The hills were beginning to green with fresh grass. After the recent shower the air was fresh and smelled of wet loam. The dome didn't have all the conveniences of the *Peloros*, but it was pleasant, and she had little cause for complaint.

Since early adolescence she had wanted to use an artist's modifier to create and record four-dimensional abstract experiences. She fulfilled her dream in a shed a hundred meters from the house, working an hour each day. In a month or so, she thought she might have something worth showing to Kawashita. Attached to the shed was a cloning laboratory with an agricultural attachment, which she was adapting for landscape and gardening purposes. That took another hour or two a day.

Next came the five years of business records to examine and assimilate. Using a tapas, she looked over the bases of her financial empire and worked out theories for improving profits and efficiency. As an adjunct to that study, she was brushing up on planetary geology, exobiology, xenopsychology, and a touch of warper science. Since she foundered on anything beyond algebra, she relied on her tapas to solve complex problems.

Still, she was restless. She didn't say anything, but it was clear Kawashita knew. She guessed she might last a year, even two, but beyond that she'd have to become active again. She watched the approaching orchestrated sunset. "I'm burned-in," she said. "Fixed and unchangeable." She turned to take another path, this leading past the truck-garden plots. A few lettuce heads were making their debut, but everything else was still dormant or undecided. An earthworm—one of sixty thousand born two weeks before—struggled on the concrete path. She reached down and carefully removed it to the soil.

Two weeks ago Kawashita had shown her a few entries from his tapas journal. They'd interested her but had been too rough and esoteric to mean much. Still, his ideas seemed to be reaching some conclusion. She hoped their schedules would coincide.

The stars came on. They were set to mimic the outside sky. A sensor on the top of the dome followed the skies closely, and if any event presented itself—meteor, aurora, or ship in orbit—the inner projector reproduced it.

"I've become awful domestic the past year," she whispered to herself. She kneeled in the dirt and sniffed the flowers on a blackthorn hedge. The routine was pleasant, her life was settled; for the first time in her memory she was content. Yet . . . not. The pressure in her throat began and moved up to squeeze a few drops of moisture from her eyes. She was afraid. If she had to leave, would he love her enough to come with her? If not, what would she do without him? They'd twined like the squash vines—separation would tear a few roots and leaves, bloody them both.

She repeated her name to herself, like some mantra of strength, but all the power had gone from it. She knew, now, of things more important than her planet-swapping career and reputation. There was peace to think about, and self-knowledge, and asking questions—probing for the sources of human corruption.

She respected Kawashita's search, but she wasn't anxious to join in on it.

It was clear what her life would be like, one way or the other. Peace would never last long. She'd always rush from goal to goal. "Dammit, that's the way I am," she said through clenched teeth. She filtered the dirt through tightened fingers. A worm, squeezed in half, wriggled out and fell to the peak of the little pile. She stood up quickly and brushed her hands on her overalls. She longed for the clean, certain corridors of her ship. Her clumsiness didn't result in any tiny slaughters there.

The dome, despite its far-reaching night sky, seemed to cramp her. Her lips worked as she half walked, half ran, to the perimeter. A honeycomb of shelves for equipment storage stood by the airlock. She chose an environment backpack and cycled through the lock. Outside she slipped on sunglasses—the planet's true time was still before sun-set—and turned up the shield's radiation filters.

The stretches of concrete were heartbreaking. They went on and on without relief, like some nightmare of infinity brought down to human terms. A few kilometers off was one tiny relief in the expanse—the Waunters' abandoned probe. She stared at it speculatively for a few minutes. Before she could reach it, dark would fall on the outside, and she didn't want to be caught on the plains at night—not again. Tomorrow, then. It would be something to look forward to.

THIRTY-SIX

Kawashita sat in the tiny rock garden, eyes closed, listening to the water splashing across the narrow streambed. Earlier in the morning he had exercised in the sandpit behind the house, swinging the silver rods, ripples forming in his tightened cheeks with the intensity of his concentration. Now he was doing in his head what he had done with his body. His thoughts shot at different targets, abstractions, conundrums, child's puzzles. He made up a few simple poems. Just as promptly, he forgot them.

That was the first stage. He then put all these aside and lulled his body into sleep with *prana-yama,* breath control. When the hands and feet were pleasantly buzzing with the total relaxation of sleep, he thought of sexual pleasure. The body's breathing increased rapidly, but it remained asleep. The past few days he had done this again and again, and found no sign of what he was looking for. Hatred didn't find much purchase in a purely sexual response. On the other hand, he could not concentrate long on violent impulses without waking himself up. He had to approach the issue at an angle, keeping the immediate impulse behind the screen.

It wasn't his purpose to meditate into a state of *samadhi.* He was purposefully keeping his ego alert, to let himself explore certain parts of his mind hidden by wakefulness. They could be called up by thinking of certain functions. When he thought of duty and discipline, the muscles in his neck and upper back tightened. There was literally a stiff neck involved. If he thought of Anna in a nonsexual context, the top of his head grew warm—a peaceful response—and he felt a pressure behind his eyes, which was ambiguous.

Then, still calm, body asleep, he asked himself particular questions and sought out their answers by pure body response. Where had Masa's dagger nicked him on the last night of the world? On the inside of the elbow. It ached briefly. He put the pain aside. Where had he landed when he'd fallen from a rock pile as a boy? His right rib cage chafed and ached. He continued until he'd mapped most of his body's memory of past injuries.

The exercises were all preparatory to assembling and posing a final series of questions, each very complex. He was trying to know himself thoroughly before he embarked on the final stage.

He'd had enough for one day. He concentrated on a point, drifted onto a higher level of uninvolved awareness, then let himself down at a chosen signal—the vibration of a toe.

After plucking a few vegetables from the garden, he went into the kitchen and prepared lunch for Anna and himself. When she didn't arrive, he ate his portion, placed hers in a holding unit, and went to find her. The dome monitor couldn't place her, so he went to the air lock. The lock light was on. He picked up a radio and held the signal button down.

"Hello," she answered. "Get a unit and come outside. I want you to take a look at this."

He slipped on a shoulder pack and cycled through the lock. The finder on the radio pointed his direction for him. He put on glasses and saw her standing on the plain beside the Waunter probe.

When he merged his field with hers near the small vehicle, she said, "It's been looking at us. At the dome, at least. See this little diode? It glows when the probe is storing up data. Why is it still looking at us?"

"Maybe it's just started. We're only majority owners, remember. The Waunters have a right to orbit and land."

"Of course. They're spying on us. We haven't looked at the recorders recently, and I haven't been paying much attention to the night sky. I'm not sure it's polite to orbit without telling us."

"Hardly a matter of etiquette," Kawashita said. "Let's go look at the recorders."

"I feel like pulling a muff over the thing," Anna said. "But no sense looking for trouble.'

"When they want to talk, they'll call. Let's go back to the dome."

THIRTY-SEVEN

In the middle of the next day's meditation, he felt the touch of an answer. It vanished for a moment, then came back with strength renewed. With every slow pulse of his heart it brightened until the light hurt the inside of his head. His breath quickened and his muscles ended their sleep.

"NO!" he shouted.

The pain stopped, but the answer remained, like a piece of iron quenched in water, not luminous but permanent. He uncrossed his legs and stood up, swinging his arms and shaking his head. He took deep breaths to loosen up his protesting body, dragged too quickly from trance. The iron-hard answer put out crystals and pointed to memories—father slapping his hands when he blamed another boy for a small house fire; mother crying for hours when he announced he was entering the military; schoolbooks with tales full of valor, brave death, God-descended history. *Women—the nonfighters—are weak; it is the triumph of man that he is built strong, so he can fight and die honorably, with calm precision and no conscious cruelty, but without quarter, without relenting, willing to inflict death on himself should he fail; forever concerned with status in society, face, honor, facing the honor of his ancestors, willing to carry that honor into the future, a vehicle for glorious victory or expunged death, for the honor of the Emperor-God, descendant of the Sun; with the precision of Buddha, like a fierce warrior donning his armor, the armor is history, the sword is faith, the strength is his years of meticulous upbringing in the supremacy of society over self . . .*

The answer spread out like an iron snowflake, sending beautiful sharp blades into all corners of his mind, each tip pointing and spearing memories, facts.

The end of Japanese history was the birth of the twentieth century in Japan. The slow, dull plodding of the Japanese people was ended by a horror they had never known, the horror of their own blindness and weakness. The blood-red sun rose over two cities; here was the new honor, the new war, no worse than the fire-death which shrank bodies into pugilistic dwarfs in Tokyo and other cities, but more precise, Buddha-like, uncompromising.

Yet the revealed weakness was not a lack of fighting strength or honor, but the weakness of clinging to all the old boats which had ferried the Japanese across so many rivers. Old conceptions, old, enchanting myths, carried out by hand and sword, hand and gun, hand and modern technology, turned into blood and ash and bits of whitened bone sticking from smoking darkness. Like a beast, the gorgeous past wrapped itself in silken folds, and when the outside blood soaked through, it had taken so long the blood was mixed with their own . . .

The answer would not be banished.

"I carried it with me," he said.

The first impulse was overwhelming. If he'd had a blade handy, he would have killed himself. Then he stepped away from the mat on the grass in horror, staring at it as if a ghost was sitting there. "I'm a robot," he said. "Rigid." He held his hands to his head. The anguish was like an incineration. He had thought the answer would bring relief, but now he faced an unacceptable, impossible solution that would neither break apart nor dissolve. It had come on him too swiftly to absorb piece by piece. All its barbs were sunk deep, growing more complex with every heartbeat.

The invisible presence on the mat waited for him. It was too old to chase after him, but now, shriveled like a mummy, its eyes were still bright. The frog-demon waited. "Clockwork warrior, clockwork leader," he said, "battling a daughter with all of history built into her. . . . Sanity didn't have a chance." He felt a chill and picked up his robe to warm him.

He had forgotten about the tapas. He picked up the palm-sized pad from the rock where he'd left it. "Reasoning mode," he said. "And speech." The screen lighted. "Argue with me," he said.

"State the argument, please."

He told the machine about the hideous answer. The tapas hummed. "It is not customary for a small unit to deal with such complex issues. You may refer to an augmented unit or connect this unit to an extension."

He put the pad down and walked into the house, to Anna's room. She was napping soundly on the sleep-field. He found the suitcase-sized extension and carried it quietly back to the rockgarden.

Connected, the pad hummed again, then listed the access numbers of banks it was going to consult.

"Just argue with me," Kawashita said. "Dissuade me."

"You fear being the slave of cultural tradition," the tapas said.

"I fear being a thing without will."

"But it is clear that all living things are bound by guidelines, some of which may not be crossed without great effort."

"What guidelines?"

"Without tecto surgery, a human may not have three arms. Without juvenates, a human may not live more than two hundred years."

"And the boundaries of the mind?"

"Large, but they exist. A human has more difficulty conceiving of warp technology than a Crocerian does. But all of these boundaries may be overcome. Humans refer the problems of visualizing higher spaces to their machines. The more choices one has, the more freedom to choose—and human extensions such as this unit were designed to expand those choices."

"But does my culture limit me? Was my heritage the cause of the evil things I allowed to happen, the evil I myself caused?"

"It is not the talent of this unit to know individual humans and their character. But if the problem is put as a theoretical—"

"Do it," Kawashita said.

"Then it is possible your actions were determined by prior cultural conditioning."

"But I won't accept lack of personal responsibility. That's a worse sin—giving in to that answer—than my original crimes."

"Explain."

"I refuse to blame the beauties of my heritage for the things I did! Or for the things any Japanese has done."

"There is something in every heritage, every philosophy, that renders it useless before certain problems."

"I don't understand."

"In time no philosophy or creed can prevent the commission of acts contrary to its sense. No creed is detailed enough to cover all the possible interpretations that can be made. Thus, Christianity brought more swords than peace, Buddhism unleashed more wars than contemplations, and the worst of any creed has been magnified. More examples can be given. The trait doesn't end with humans. Living beings are too complex to be encompassed by any single set of rules."

"But why do men choose to be perverse? Why are some weak, others strong? Why did I fail?"

"This unit is specifically enjoined against attempting further answers."

Kawashita stammered for a moment. He'd never heard a tapas refuse to answer. "What enjoins you?"

"This unit senses the upset state of the questioner and suggests he speak with another human. This unit is specifically enjoined against acting as a psychiatrist."

Kawashita clenched his fists and lifted them in fury. "I don't request psychiatric help! I just want to know why we do the things we do!" The tapas hummed. "Damn you, don't lock up on me! I'll put the question differently . . ." But no matter how he phrased it, the tapas merely hummed. He picked up the pad and attached case and swung them against a wall. "Damn all these things," he muttered in Japanese, shoulders stooped, arms hanging at his sides. "All my learning. Nothing has helped me. Half-answers . . . I don't even know the proper questions." He held one hand to his forehead, palm to skin, and leaned his head back. "I have to go to the source," he said. "The *kami*. They must know." His hand came away damp with sweat.

Outside, the day sky was up in the dome. He could see a few stars even so, and the moving point of the Waunter's ship—but it was a machine's interpretation. Somewhere sensors were relaying the heaven's patterns. Wherever the *kami* had gone, they might still try to reach him, to explain. And he wouldn't have their answers interpreted by machines. The damned things would all lock up on him at the crucial moment.

He picked up a box and stuffed a few provisions into it—a piece of fruit from the garden, some vegetables left over from dinner the night before, a handful of cooked rice. He carried the box under one arm, crossing the compound to the gate in the stone wall. He swung the gate wide. Behind him something started beeping, and voices spoke throughout the house.

It was important to ask his questions outside. He ran across the lawn and through the young forest, under the peristyle roof to the air lock.

"Open," he ordered. The door swung wide and he stepped into the chamber. "Cycle."

"This unit cannot cycle unless the occupants are adequately protected by environment packages or suits."

"Cycle! I gave an order!"

"This unit—"

He ran outside and picked up a stone, then returned to the lock and hammered at the light, which indicated a vox mechanism was working. "Let . . . me . . . out . . . now!" The rock smashed the light, but the air lock stayed closed.

"Yoshio!" someone called. He ignored it.

He was kicking the door with the sides of his bare feet, bruising them and splitting the skin, when Nestor ran up, her gown swirling. "Yoshio! Stop, please stop!" She grabbed at him, and he turned to her, glaring.

"You all try to stop me. Everything is misleading, fouling my mind! Impure! All the progress, all the learning, makes my brain rot with disgust!"

Nestor backed off. "Med unit," she said. Yoshio returned to kicking the lock door. "It won't let you out unless you put on a suit," she said. "Where do you want to go?"

"Out to speak," he said. "Everything stops me."

"You're just forgetting, there's not much air outside. You can't ask questions if there's no air to breathe. Nothing will hear you, and you'll die anyway before you get an answer. Who are you going to ask?"

"The *kami*, the stars."

"Then it's best to use a transmitter, don't you think? Reach them much quicker, wherever they are."

Kawashita looked at her sadly. "Anna," he said. "It's all going wrong."

"I know, I know." She wiped tears from her eyes. "It's been too much. You asked too much of yourself."

"Never too much! I'm a *warrior!*" He pushed away from the hatch and tried to kick the hatch again, but lost his balance and fell to the floor with a sickening jolt. "I am not weak, I make up my own mind. I'm an individual, and I can do what I will . . ." he said in harsh gasps. He lifted his head up, then let it fall back.

"MED UNIT!" Anna screamed. The sphere and two cubes floated up. "Don't make him sleep, don't impair CNS, just calm him down."

When they were done, Yoshio stared at nothing, his lips moving. His eyes focused on Anna, and he smiled at her faintly. "My love," he said. "All that I love, all that I believe." The cubes dropped arms and gently lifted him back to the house.

THIRTY-EIGHT

On the fourth day of orbit the circling hawk decided to come down. Anna stood outside the dome, watching the lander's star fall, then grow larger and rise, then seem to sit motionless in the sky. It was describing a graceful curve, getting brighter every second. The last few instants of its flight it seemed to burn, plunging toward the concrete, leaving a trail of cloud and glowing air. It touched down gently as a feather.

She sealed the air lock and walked under the peristyle roof into the light of dome day. Her hand reached down to the signaling sensors and flipped off the alarm. In the house Kawashita sat on a cushion, looking out the open doors at the rock garden. "They're down," she said. "How do you feel?"

"Better," he answered. "I'm sorry—"

"You've already apologized twice. That's enough. And nothing to apologize for, unless you say it to your foot, or your ankle, or the lump on your skull."

"You are angry."

"I am. Not at you—not just at you, anyway. At everything. The *Peloros* won't be back for a week. Until then, we're stuck. No way out, and *them* outside."

"You worry about the Waunters?"

"I don't know. They didn't answer our transmissions, didn't even send notice to our orbit sensors."

"Perhaps their ship isn't equipped to send."

"Listeners? Don't be silly."

"So we wait."

"I'm sick of waiting. Waiting for you to finally crack up, feeling my back tingle every time I wonder if they've landed or not . . . sick of not knowing why I'm so anxious."

"I have abused you," Kawashita said. "Expected too much from you."

"Shit," Anna said. "I'm a rock as far as that goes, but I have the right to be irritated, don't I? I don't like seeing your goddamned quest tear you apart. Save me from saints and revolutionaries!"

Kawashita stood and flexed his legs in the shaft of light coming through the doors. "I am calm now. It won't happen again. I didn't know I could be dangerous."

Nestor held her hand to her mouth and bit lightly at her knuckles. "I'm glad to hear it's over," she said. "You'd start me biting my nails again."

"I don't think it's over, but I won't be violent again. I think I see why I call the Perfidisians *kami*. They can't be like you and me, not like the Aighors, the Crocerians. They're something else, in another category."

"I won't dispute that. If anyone has a right to a theory, you do. But how are you going to face yourself? I mean, that's what you've been after, isn't it?"

"I can face myself without knowing all the answers. I'm not the one to know—but the Perfidisians, they know for me."

Anna sat down and held both hands in her lap. "Are you done here?"

Kawashita smiled. "Poor restless Anna. Anxious to get on with things."

"Well?"

"Yes. We can go wherever we want. They aren't here anymore."

She took a deep breath. "We both took risks," she said. "I'm surprised we made it this far."

The radio chimed and they went into the equipment shed to answer it. "This unit has a message from Alae and Oomalo Waunter," the device said. "They request permission to visit and talk."

"It's domestic," Kawashita said, grinning at her. "They've come to visit."

"They're not the casual type. But I suppose we're obliged to talk to them. I'll answer," she told the unit. "Nestor here. What can we do for you?"

"Greetings, madam. This is Oomalo Waunter. We've come to discuss transferring deed to our share of the planet's profits. When can we meet with you?"

"Whenever you wish, Mr. Waunter. We have no set schedules here."

"Then my wife and I will be at the dome entrance in an hour. We have to store our probe first—forgot it in the rush last time."

"We await." She switched the radio off and shook her head. "Who the hell would buy a ten-percent share of eventual profits for this place?"

"A fool, or a far-sighted speculator. We're inviting them inside?"

"We'll talk for an hour—that should be enough—then show them out. They're not my favorite people."

THIRTY-NINE

"It's beautiful—really remarkable, what you've done here," Oomalo Waunter said. His wife agreed with a nod and tight smile.

"Thank you," Anna said. "It passes the time. My husband is sleeping now. He had a bad fall yesterday."

"Oh?" Alae said.

"So I'll conduct the business. There's a table under the tree"—she pointed—"and it's very pleasant to sit in the shade."

"Do you have an affidavit from Mr. Kawashita stating you're empowered to conduct his business?" Oomalo asked. Anna didn't show a glimmer of irritation.

"As his wife, I'm legally empowered without any affidavit, so long as he gives recorded and witnessed approval before final dispensation."

"Of course."

"So—what are the circumstances?"

"We plan to settle down on a colony world, sell the ship, sell our holdings here—is this being recorded?"

"Of course not," Anna lied.

"We don't want certain people to be able to trace us," Alae said. Oomalo's grin shifted a notch, but he held it firm and continued. "We need to build up enough capital to see us through the next couple of centuries. We're not Abstainers, you know, so we have to make our plans way ahead of time."

"I see," Anna said. "Do you have a buyer?"

"The purchasers wish to remain anonymous. We'll represent their concerns until the deal is final."

"What's the bid?"

"We're not at liberty to discuss that with you. They're quite interested, however."

"I can't consent to the deal until I know who the purchaser is, and what's being bid."

"You can't interfere with our attempt to sell," Alae said, cocking her head to one side, eyes wide.

"It seems the provisions of the contract conflict here—" Oomalo began.

"No," Anna said calmly, "not at all. Read it carefully. Majority holder has the right to approve any changes in ownership which might affect his holdings. We can't interfere with your attempt to set up a deal—but if you want any sale to go through Centrum files, we must know the particulars. We'll be circumspect, of course."

Alae sighed with irritation. "Well," Oomalo said, "I think we can trust you. Hafkan Bestmerit is interested in buying our share."

"Very good," Anna said. "They're tough characters to negotiate with. And their bid?"

"Option of seven billion, royalties of one degree, considerations for twelve million."

"More than a fair offer," Anna said. "I doubt they'll make anything off the deal. There's nothing here."

"I'm not sure that's been determined yet," Alae said sharply. Anna shook her head.

"I'm convinced, my husband is convinced. But if Hafkan Bestmerit isn't, that's all to your advantage."

"Final word should come through in the next few days." Oomalo took a deep breath and looked across the low hills. "It's really quite pleasant here. We're having difficulties with some instruments in our lander. Do you have replacements for a DN65 inertial guidance rotor?"

"None to spare," Anna said.

"How long before your ship returns?"

She caught herself before answering. "Any time now."

"Would it be possible to purchase one from your lander? I'm sure you have several redundant systems—but our craft is much older . . ."

"As I said, none to spare."

"No lander," Oomalo said. "Of course not. Where would you go? I'm being silly. But that puts us in a fix. Without that rotor, we'd take a substantial risk trying to get back to the ship. I hope you won't mind if we stay here until your ship returns? If it's no imposition."

Anna tapped her fingers on the table, pausing before

saying, "No. No imposition. We have a small building not far from here which should hold you comfortably."

"Are there any animals?" Alae asked.

"Only insects. They won't bother you."

"I think we're a bit premature, approaching you before everything is worked out. But we expected to receive the transmission on the way. If Alae could get some of our things from the lander, we'll take advantage of your hospitality and rest for a while. Then, may we cook you dinner? I'm sure your foodstuffs are preferable to our own—but I'm a fair cook, and Alae does wonderful things with hydroponic materials."

"Of course," Anna said. She followed them to the air lock and stood talking with Oomalo while his wife walked back to the lander. The man was too smooth, too relaxed. He made her nervous. His calmness didn't seem to have the same source as her own—a mask used while conducting business. The business seemed to mean very little to him.

"She's coming back now," Waunter said, watching the outer hatch light come on. "This is really very kind of you. We're used to much bigger spaces than a lander affords."

"Not at all. I'm sure you have lots to tell us—stories about your experiences, how you found the planet deserted . . . keep us very entertained."

What would she carry in the luggage? Was there any way to detect it? The lock sensors—but not with Oomalo watching. Why was she worried? *Calm.* If they were planning, it was best to appear unsuspecting.

"We're not very used to company ourselves," Oomalo was saying. "Living alone for so many years. I can adjust, but my wife may not react in the most acceptable manner." He smiled. His smile, Anna thought, was really quite genuine and warm. When it wasn't used, however, Oomalo's face became a waxy blank, eyes bright and observing but somehow insulated.

Alae stood in the lock. She was carrying a cloth travel bag. "Just a few things. We won't be here long."

Yoshio met them on the path to the compound. He was dressed in blue coveralls and carried a piece of paper on which he drew curved and straight lines. He held up his scriber in greeting and shook Alae's hand, nodding to

Oomalo. "Welcome back," he said. "I trust things have gone well for you."

Alae shrugged. "We still have to sell out."

"We were used to having one employer and steady work," Oomalo explained. "We were free-lancers only technically . . . and the reality, so soon, was hard for a while. But we're getting by. Aren't we, Alae?"

The woman nodded, looking between Kawashita and Nestor. Anna instinctively turned to see what she was staring at—nothing but a hedgerow. A small shiver wriggled up her back. "They're staying for dinner," she said.

The meal was highly spiced, not to Anna's taste. Kawashita ate it without comment. He said very little. The dome evening settled onto the open patio.

Oomalo dominated the evening's talk. Anna thought his quest for hidden artifacts on the Aighor ship was compulsive, but she listened intently to his description of the old guidance systems and computers.

Alae sat as quiet as Kawashita, face expressionless. Everything was cordial, but Anna could not relax.

She escorted the Waunters to their shed, followed a few yards behind by Kawashita, who still clutched his piece of paper and scriber.

On the way back to the house, she cursed softly. "We haven't got *anything*," she said. "No weapons, no escape . . . damn!"

"You're worried about them. Why?"

"Their story falls apart every time I come close to it. Who would buy this place? Certainly not the Hafkan Bestmerit negotiators. If they were interested, they'd contact us first—money is no object to them, since most don't use it the way we do, anyway. So I ask myself why the Waunters are here, and—I don't know! I've told them the ship will be back anytime now, but they know we're alone here. We need something—the garden tools, something from the shed. A cutter."

Kawashita held his hand to his head and frowned. "Yes. One for each of us."

"What's the matter?"

"The bruise."

"Do you want a med unit?"

"No. Just a throb. It's gone now."

"Tools from the shed. Two cutters—anything more

powerful? Can we remove the torches from the welders? No. Power supply is too big. Anything else?"

He shook his head.

"And let's not get separated while they're here. We should stay within sight of each other at all times. Let's go into the garden." He followed and stood in the cricket-filled dusk while she rummaged in the shed. "Carry it in your pocket," she said as she came out. She showed him how to collapse the handle of the pistol-shaped tool.

"When it's folded, it won't work. To unfold it, push this button, and to release the safety, push again. I'm going to do something illegal here. Donatien taught me this a long time ago, along with general lessons in dirty fighting. When the handle is partially collapsed, a gap appears between the upper grip and the body—here, see? There's a small brain in the cutter which decides whether or not activating the tool will harm an animal. If it thinks it will, the cutter shuts down temporarily. The sensor wires are on one side of the gap—but if we cut them, it just deactivates the whole tool. We can, however, smash the brain with a short blade." She took out a pocket knife and performed the operation on both cutters.

"Now look. My cutter is on, set to three inches. I'm going to slice my finger a bit." The glowing field nudged her index finger and drew a drop of blood. "It'll extend to twenty feet and cut flesh down to bone—but it won't cut through bone. It's a small garden tool, not set for anything tougher than a wood stem. So aim at someone's throat, or the abdomen, and remember—the field is rigid. It extends across twenty feet, but it'll take quite a swing to cut anything at the extreme end. It's best at edge-cutting, and not very good at puncturing."

Kawashita folded the altered cutter and put it in his pocket.

"Promise me you'll be careful," Anna said.

"Everything will be fine." He smiled.

"Are you feeling all right?"

"Not super, but I'll do." He walked back to the house, moving slowly from side to side on the path. He stopped once and bent to pick a handful of rye grass, sniffing it.

"Why give lessons to an old warrior?" she asked herself aloud. "He's the one should be lecturing *me*." But something was still wrong with him. She shook her head. Holding the cutter tightly, she swung around on impulse and activated the field. She swept through a row of irises, cleanly severing the purple flowers. Then she folded the tool and put it in her waist pocket, checking to see if it made a bulge. The outside didn't look much different from a tapas.

Later, in her sleep-field, with Kawashita in a lotus position on his mattress, she closed her eyes and tried to relax. It was possible she was being too jumpy. Their excuses for getting into the dome were on the edge of believability, and Alae had opened her bag wide enough several times for Anna to see there were no large weapons in it. But a persistent voice said, *Knife . . . wire . . . don't let them near. . . .*

Still, it was business. She'd conducted business before under worse circumstances.

The house and compound were surrounded by sensor nets. For the moment they were secure. She rolled over and looked at Kawashita. He was drawing on his piece of paper again—straight lines, curves, squiggles. There was a circle in the middle of the page, and all the lines radiated from it. "What are you drawing?" she asked.

"Where we haven't been," he said.

She nodded and lay on her back. A kind of numbness crept over her. Who was crazier, Yoshio or herself?

In the morning the communications equipment announced a message from the *Peloros.* Anna listened to it before waking Kawashita, who had stayed up far into the night. As she bent over to shake him, his eyes came open and he stared at her. His whole body had tensed as she approached. Now he grinned and relaxed. "What was that all about?" she asked.

"Alert," he said. "You tell me to be aware."

"We're okay in the house, alone. The ship says it'll be here in three days. Are you willing to leave by then?"

Yoshio scowled and looked at his paper. "I don't know," he said. "Perhaps. But I have to go outside with the cart first."

"Okay. We'll take the Waunters with us—can't leave them in here alone. A group journey."

"No," he said.

"I don't trust them anywhere but in their lander, or right with us."

"I have no fear of them, but I should not be disturbed by too many people. One can come—I will watch out for myself."

"We shouldn't separate," Anna said doggedly. "Don't you understand?"

"You underestimate me," Kawashita said, sitting up and putting on his robe. "I slept with one eye open for many years, remember?"

"You haven't been feeling well."

"I'll admit that. But I'm still alert. And I'm much closer to figuring out the puzzle."

"The paths?"

"Yes. Statistics, distributions."

"I don't see what you're after."

"You'll understand."

The compound sensors announced intruders. Anna went into the rock garden to meet them and offer breakfast, and Yoshio came out in coveralls. The meal was quiet, less relaxed than the night before. Alae commented on the garden's precision. "I admire a solid view of things," she said softly. "Things in their place, all's right in the mind."

"Japanese tradition," Anna said. "Tranquility of the surroundings, tranquil thoughts."

"Yes. I can see that," Alae said. "Certainties."

"We were wondering what it's like to live here," Oomalo said. "This isn't exactly a choice world—I say that despite our share in it—and surely both of you have lived in better surroundings. Yoshio lived in a better time, and Anna . . . well." He smiled.

"It's interesting. We're always coming up with surprises," Yoshio said.

"Oh?" Alae looked up.

"Anna has found she doesn't like going out after dark."

"You were a bit upset, too," Anna said.

"We both feel the pressure of something unidentifiable outside. Ghosts, perhaps? At any rate, there's a lot more than meets the eye, and when the dark takes away the eye's dominion, it becomes more obvious."

"You think there are artifacts?" Oomalo asked. Alae's face became animated, and she followed her husband's question with a silent movement of her lips.

Kawashita shook his head. "Probably not. Everything has been searched, and the Perfidisians were too thorough.

But, like you and your ship," he looked at Oomalo, "I can't quite give up hoping."

"Look at all of us," Alae said. "Spending our lives chasing after the garbage of the past. Wasted information, wasted debris . . . very foolish. No certainty at all, no neatness even."

Anna was startled by the woman's concise evaluation. "A syndrome," she said, nodding in agreement. "Shall we invent a name for it?"

"I think Yoshio and I would disagree with you women," Oomalo said. "It adds richness to life . . . an expectation. The potential of discovery is what keeps all good people working."

"Still, it's crazy," Kawashita admitted. His fingers folded and unfolded the piece of paper. Oomalo dropped his glance every time the drawing was fully revealed, examining it closely. "I am going for a walk," the Japanese said, standing up suddenly. Anna started to say something, but closed her mouth and clenched her teeth.

"Outside?" Alae asked.

"Something has occurred to me," he continued.

"What's that?" Oomalo asked.

"I'm not certain. Anna, will you come with me?"

"We'd better stay in here."

"Nonsense, the weather's fine outside," Oomalo said. "Do you need company?"

"No," Kawashita said. Anna tried to catch his gaze but couldn't. A sharp taste began at the back of her throat.

"I'll go along," she said.

"There are some questions I'd like to ask, things we might decide more easily if we had some quiet," Oomalo said to her. "Alae has preparations to make on the lander, and we could—"

"Are you taking a cart?" Alae asked Kawashita. "Perhaps I could hitch a ride."

"I think we'd better stay here, all of us," Anna said.

"Why?" Alae asked sharply.

"We can get the negotiations done more quickly," Anna said lamely.

"I'll ride out with your husband and walk back. We can talk just an hour or so from now."

Anna felt like shouting but kept her outward calm. This was too pat, too obvious . . . and yet, unless she deliberately accused them of planning foul play—and perhaps forced their hand, made them even more dangerous—she had no argument worth voicing. And if her fears were groundless, she'd be a fool, accused of inhospitality at the very least. That might be a perfectly reasonable exchange for safety. But her suspicions couldn't override her caution. This morning Yoshio had demonstrated that he was alert, capable. He could probably handle Alae without trouble, and she was evenly matched against Oomalo.

Reluctantly, she watched Kawashita and Alae walk to the peristyle. Oomalo sat in his chair, finishing the last of a glass of fresh juice. "This is very good," he said, licking his lips. "Quite refreshing."

FORTY

Kawashita said nothing to the woman beside him on the cart. He was concentrating on steering. When he tried to turn it in one direction . . .

He forgot making the effort. But now something was lingering behind the erased memory. Somewhere a persuasive force was weakening. He tried to turn the cart aside again and felt a tug in his head, directing him to another course. The tug was more obvious as they approached the Waunters' lander. "What's the matter?" Alae asked.

"Something's wrong."

"Can I help?"

"I can only go a certain number of ways."

"What do you mean?"

"Something limits our pathways, stops us from going off given courses."

"But there's nothing here."

He held up his hand and motioned for her to take the wheel. She did so, the cart sped up again, and she maneuvered it back and forth. "Goes anyway I want it to," she said.

Kawashita shook his head, irritated. "But you aren't pulling it where it *shouldn't* go. Try . . . here."

They both forgot. He shook his head to clear it. Alae stared ahead as if nothing had happened. "What?" she asked.

"We're here," he said, indicating the lander. "I must go farther."

"If it's so important, I can go with you." She was clearly as excited as he was, but it seemed for different reasons. He was in too much of a hurry to argue. He spun the cart around and set it on automatic pilot, then examined his chart. When he snapped out of the lull of forgetfulness again, the paper was on the floor of the cart, almost falling out. He bent to pick it up. Their direction had changed, but he wasn't sure how. He didn't try to change the cart's course again until they were six kilometers from the dome. This time he distinctly remembered giving the order to his arm muscles to turn the wheel. And he remembered the arms refusing. He slammed the cart to a halt. Alae almost fell out, cursing. Something clattered by the edge of the seat cushion, but he didn't look to see what it was.

Alae did. She was frightened by his irrational behavior. When he stepped out of the cart, she did, too. Their environment fields separated with a faint *plop*. Then she saw the folded cutter on the floor of the cart. She picked it up, adjusted it, and nicked her finger accidentally. She swore, too low for Kawashita to hear.

If the cart wouldn't turn, he reasoned, something was in its way. If he stepped from the desired path, he would encounter whatever the obstacle was.

He held out his hands. Sweat broke out on his forehead. Whatever the persuasive force was, it was weakening. Just as the weather machines had weakened and collapsed, just as the environment in the dome had finally given out, a last device was fading.

Alae watched him with dismay. He was acting like a madman. Or he was trying a ruse on her, to catch her off guard. "Yes," she said to herself, "kill me, get rid of both of us." She turned to look at the dome. She wanted to warn Oomalo, but it was too late.

FORTY-ONE

It was all out in the open now. "What are we going to do, then?" Nestor asked.

"Be more direct, I hope," Oomalo said. "I'd like both of you to accompany us in the lander. It's silly wasting your time. You're such a powerful and intelligent woman—silly wasting all that here. Neither of you wants to give it all up—your lives, everything, for this stupid world."

"What'll happen in the lander?"

"My wife and your husband will be there. We're all partners in this venture. You've tried to hide something, but we know now, and we'll just take our fair share."

Anna looked for some sign of insanity in the man but couldn't find any. He was calm, rational, and seemed to be following a plan.

"I don't know what the hell you're talking about."

"We have good evidence you've found artifacts here. We intend to get our share of the sale of any such finds. That's legal. We're prepared to use slightly illegal means, however, to convince you."

"Legal or illegal, I don't know what you're talking about. We haven't found anything here since the first landings. Who's been telling you these lies?"

"That doesn't matter now. Alae—"

"What's she doing to Yoshio? Have you got something planned?"

"Things are working out fine as they are. Your husband is strange."

Anna laughed.

"We're serious. We lost just about everything we valued when this place turned into a bust. We have nothing more to lose, and a lot more to gain. We're taking you back to our ship." He reached into his collar and drew out a tiny sliver of silvery metal.

"What's that?"

"It's Crocerian. Our employers—our original employers—provided them in case we should get in trouble at our post. The Aighor ship wasn't allowed to have registered weapons. We weren't rich enough to have a few rulings reversed. These will do, however. Alae has one."

"Yoshio isn't well—he took a fall several days ago."

"We have med units on the ship."

Anna shook her head. "I don't believe this," she said. "You're everything I thought, you'd be. Everything! I shouldn't have even let you land."

"We were prepared for that, too."

"What will you do when my ship finds we're gone? Hold us for ransom?"

"No. They won't know where you are, and we won't tell them. We'll just keep you until you tell us what you've found, and make a recorded confession."

"We haven't found *anything*!" Anna shouted. "Oomalo brought up the sliver.

"Be calm," he said. "I'm calm. Nothing will go wrong." He pointed to the peristyle and the air lock. "We'll put on environment packs and walk to the lander. Let go."

FORTY-TWO

Kawashita faced the unseen barrier with a frown. He placed one hand on apparently empty air and pushed.

"What are you doing?" Alae asked. She stood five paces behind him, fingering the cutter.

He didn't answer. He backed away and felt the pressure stop. The illusion, the restraints, were slowly letting up. Two days ago none of them could have even considered leaving the assigned pathways. Now, with an effort of will, at least he could do so. He squinted and saw a few patches of fog.

"See anything?" he asked.

"Nothing. What are you doing?"

"There's a wall or building here. We can't see it. But something is changing. If I concentrate, I can see it a little and feel it."

"Who are you trying to fool? You knew there was something here, you knew it the day we met. You planned it all from the beginning, to keep us out, keep us away from what we deserve. And then you arm yourself to kill us." She didn't bother to remove the sliver from her collar. She extended the cutter's field.

Kawashita looked over his shoulder at her and felt the slice across his arm. He held his hand against the blood and winced at the searing pain. He forced his watering eyes open and stepped back against the invisible wall. Alae gritted her teeth and moved in to finish her work.

FORTY-THREE

They stood in the air lock, Oomalo behind her, waiting for the cycle to complete. Their fields came on simultaneously.

"Out," he said. They walked away from the dome.

At first the ground looked like it was covered by mist. Then the mist began to rise, filled with captured rainbows, forming walls, then buildings, then blocking their view of the lander. A city rose around them, ancient and decrepit, walls collapsed, rubble scattered. Oomalo twirled around and shouted something. Anna shut her eyes for a moment and reached into her pocket. He was facing away from her as she extended the field and cut the back of his hand. The sliver dropped. He screamed and rushed to merge their envelopes. The second swipe caught him in the neck, and he swayed, then went down, clutching at the gash, taking the cutting tool with him.

She started screaming and calling Yoshio's name.

FORTY-FOUR

Transcription of all-body record:

The pain and darkness are complete. He is on his back, staring at the dark blue sky, watching stars move and fall one by one, then return. Like universes dying and being born. Then the images steady and the pain subsides. "Hello," Yoshio says. "Where is she? What did she do to me?"

He thinks he hears somebody speaking, but he can't see anyone around him. He can't see the woman who cut him. He can see a spreading pool of blood, and feel a bitter taste in his mouth, and hear the voice—and there are buildings all around—but nothing makes any sense.

Then his hearing clears.

"Who would you have us be? We did not judge, only studied."

"What?"

"Your reactions told us what we needed to know."

"Where are you?"

"We conclude our final experiment. You have been curious to know what we are and where we come from. There is no need to conceal the answers now. We are not another species; we are not even self-aware by your standards. We are simply 'agents' created to represent another group of beings. Only a few species will be able to survive the end of this universe and seed the next."

"Have I been worthy?" Kawashita asks. "Why come back and tell me these things?"

"It is apparent that human beings represent no threat to

our creators, our interests. You have basic flaws which will prevent you from finishing in the competition. You will attempt to create your own agent, but you won't understand why, or the functions it must serve, and you will destroy it. Knowing this, we have no further curiosity. You have done well in your thoughts and researches. No more could have been expected, for your circumstances were extraordinary. It is unfortunate that your very nature as a human being has prevented you from reaching your goal. But full understanding is a thing granted to few species, much less individuals.

"The Perfidisians have never been. Now even their illusion passes on."

The stars fade and fall again. He sits quiet, lips working. "Not *kami*," he says. "You took me, you needed me to fail, to make the experiment fulfill . . . I was not wanting! I was not failing. Everything possible . . ."

He closes his eyes, takes a deep, shuddering breath, and opens them again.

"But you are wrong," he says. "Very, very *wrong*." He takes out the tapas and tries to smash it on the concrete. After three swings, the recording stops, but not because he has damaged the machine.

FORTY-FIVE

Jason DiNova leaned over the body of Oomalo Waunter and shook his head. "My God, what happened here?" he whispered. The man's neck had almost been cut through. He picked up the slender piece of metal near Waunter's hand and examined it.

"What's that?" Kondrashef asked.

"A Crocerian weapon. Illegal, I think."

"What were they trying to do?"

"Kill Anna. They must have tried to kill her." DiNova looked at the dome entrance, then at the surrounding ruins. "I don't believe all this."

Oliphant's voice came over the radio in Kondrashef's environment pack. "We've found Anna. We need a medical unit and transport."

"Is she hurt?" DiNova asked, standing beside the body.

"Not physically, no. But she's half out of her mind. Keeps calling for Alae Waunter. She found Kawashita—"

"How is he?"

"Dead," Oliphant said. "Somebody killed him with an altered cutting tool."

"Why?" DiNova asked, dazed.

"Two crazy independents," Kondrashef said.

They brought the medical unit and a second cart out of the dome and followed a clear stretch between the ruins. Kondrashef helped pick up Kawashita's body and put it in the back. The medical unit floated ahead.

Oliphant stood by Anna Nestor. She was clutching a tapas pad, silent, looking at the ground. DiNova joined them and urged Anna to return to the ship as soon as possible. She walked away without argument, climbing into the cart, reaching out to touch the bag that held her husband.

"We've got to find Alae Waunter," DiNova told Oliphant.

"Not a trace of her," the young officer said. "I've had two men with sensors out tracking for an hour, ever since we arrived. Nothing."

"What about the buildings? Where did they come from?"

Oliphant shrugged. "They must have been here all the time. They're stripped, nothing but extrusions of the concrete."

DiNova shook his head, not for the last time that day. "I don't believe all this."

Addendum to this record:

"Yoshio, I'm ninety now. Sixty-one years I've been coming to this planet, once a year, to visit you. I still think about you . . . about what you found. They *were* wrong, you know. You were proof by example. They left us nothing but the old shells of abandoned laboratories, where they must have examined millions of others, as they did you— for how many millions of years? We may never know.

"But they were wrong. If it takes my whole life, I'll prove them wrong. I vow this each time I visit you. Well, I haven't found them yet. But in the end, when all is said and done, we'll meet them on equal ground. And I hope we still know how to sneer.

"I think they're still around. You knew they were. But my advisers look upon that view as unworthy of comment. Old, rusty Anna still ticking over about past grief. No matter.

"Dear Yoshio, each time . . . You've got me crying again. I miss you very, very much. I've put a piece of ribbon in your shrine. You are *kami* to me now.

"And every day I say 'Hello!' "